Forever Love

By

Elizabeth Castle

Name: Castle, Elizabeth, author

Title: Forever Love

Description: Series: The Heart's Way Book 4

Publisher: In The Air Publishing

Identifiers: ISBN 9781967731183 (ebook) | ISBN 9781967731190 (paperback) | ISBN 9798305656855 (amazon hardcover)

Cover Designer: betibup33

Chapter One

Ellis Wallace sat in the corner of the room, watching the festivities going on around him. He would have skipped the wedding, but Lindsay had pleaded with him when he'd declined her wedding invitation. He wasn't sure why his ex-fiancée wanted him to attend her wedding, but he always did have a problem saying no to her. They hadn't been a real couple in ten years, hadn't been lovers in five, and hadn't spoken for the past year and a half. He hadn't known it, but that's when she'd gotten engaged. But when she'd shown up at his office asking him to please attend, he'd found himself agreeing. Of course, that had been before he'd been shot.

This was the second wedding he'd attended in the past month. The first had been his employer's wedding. He was happy she'd found happiness with her new husband Carter. Though he'd still been in a lot of pain, he wouldn't have missed that wedding for the world. Selena had not only been his employer for the past six years, but she was also his friend. And as of a month ago, he was her vice president instead of her bodyguard. Though he never imagined himself in the role of a corporate executive, he now held the title. And once his body stopped hurting and he could stay on his feet without tiring, it would be in fact, and not just in title.

So here he was at his ex's wedding, sitting in the corner, wishing he could crawl into his bed and stay there. The bullet that had torn through his upper chest was the one that bothered him the most. Scar tissue had formed, but beneath the surface of the knotted scar tissue, he could still feel where the bullet had torn through, missing his spine by a mere half inch. The bullet had also missed his heart. His lung hadn't been so lucky, but all in all, he had lucked out. Three bullets, almost point-blank range, had managed to do very little damage to his internal organs. A nicked liver, a hole in his lung, and a slug lodged in his left arm were what he got for his troubles. But he was being paid to protect Selena with his life. It had very nearly cost him that.

About an hour into the reception, Ellis started wondering if it was too soon to make his exit. He'd listened to a toast, eaten rubbery, flavorless chicken, and drunk the glass of champagne put in front of him. He wasn't interested in the overly decorated cake that was currently taking center stage. He figured that, as the ex-fiancé, he had more than fulfilled whatever obligation he had to the bride.

But before Ellis could struggle to his feet, he saw her. He thought he had caught a glimpse of her earlier but thought it must have been his imagination. There was no way Olivia Knight was attending the biggest social event of the year. His ex, Lindsay, was now married to a Hollywood producer. Lindsay didn't come from a wealthy background, but she hung around some very influential people, and with some careful investing, investing he had done for her, she was now a wealthy woman. Anyone who thought they were someone tried to get an invitation to this wedding. Olivia was a cybersecurity agent with a PI firm. The firm was one of the most well-known agencies in the country, but Olivia was just another cog in the wheel, no one special. So what was she doing here?

But as he strained to get a better look at the woman in the darkened ballroom, he realized Olivia was indeed a guest at the party. She wore a black dress with a slit up the left leg. If he wasn't mistaken, it was the same dress she'd worn to Selena's wedding, where she had been working as a security guard. He'd been furious to see her working out on the front lines instead of behind her computer.

Ellis didn't consider himself old-fashioned, but Olivia wasn't cut out to be a bodyguard. Jack, her employer and his friend, had informed him that Olivia wanted to get out from behind her desk. As a previous employee of Jack and as his friend, he'd felt no compunction telling him to get her back where she belonged. Jack's eyes had danced with humor, and he hadn't followed Ellis's advice.

Instead of leaving the reception, Ellis leaned further back in his chair and watched Olivia as she made rounds through the ballroom. He didn't have a hard time spotting her. She stood out like a sore thumb. The women attending the reception were wearing thousands of dollars in jewels and gowns with designer labels. Their hair was styled and lacquered in place, not a strand allowed to stray. Olivia was quite the opposite. She wore a plain black dress paired with nothing more than a pair of black high-heeled sandals. Her hair was loose and flowing down her back in waves. She'd let it grow out over the past year, and it was now halfway down her back. He had to admit he approved.

Olivia looked like an average California blonde. Her honey-blonde hair was bleached from hours spent under the sun. Her skin glowed with a natural tan. Her bright blue eyes finished off the California blonde look. He supposed she looked very girl-next-door. He preferred brunettes, the more exotic the better. The last woman he'd dated had been from Brazil. Her honey-toned skin had been accompanied by exotic brown eyes and thick black hair that fell to her waist. She'd come to California to be an actress, as so many other young women did. But Natália had ended up with a modeling contract instead and had found success. He'd met her through his work, as he did most of the women he dated. Whatever social events Selena attended, he also attended. And if the venue allowed it, he'd do a little socializing himself. He was well paid for his services, and he looked the part of a rich, successful businessman. And he supposed his hard edges attracted as many women as they deterred.

It still puzzled him why he had a hard time getting Olivia out of his mind. She wasn't his type. He'd met her a year ago when he'd been working on a case for Selena. Selena was a successful antiquities dealer, and she owned a huge corporation that specialized in various antiquities and artifacts. She also helped catch those who were involved in the underbelly of the antiquities trade. There had been one particular case where Selena had enlisted Jack's help. Both he and Selena had other matters to attend to, so Jack had sent them Olivia. Jack claimed she was the best computer hacker he had, and that Olivia had some experience tracing missing property. Jack hadn't elaborated on what that property had been, but both Ellis and Selena trusted Jack's judgment.

Olivia had been difficult and prickly the entire time she had been working under him. Ellis admitted his first problem had been with her looks. She had shown up at Powell Trading on her first day on the job wearing a pair of white capris and a tank top, paired with a pair of cheap sandals. She'd not been wearing any makeup, and her damp, sun-streaked hair had been pulled back in a ponytail. She'd hardly looked the part of a professional investigator. She'd looked more like she'd just come from the beach.

His second issue with her had been her attitude. She'd taken one look at him and dismissed him. She'd asked him to show her where the investigation team was so she could get started. When he'd told her he was the lead investigator on the project, she'd looked down her nose at him, brushed past him into Selena's office, and asked Selena if she was really supposed to work with the macho man standing behind her. Selena had been taken aback at first; then she had smiled at the woman. Selena assured Olivia that Ellis was the right man and not to let the slick hair and fancy suit throw her off her game.

And when he was feeling honest, his third and final problem with Olivia was that despite her casual appearance and feisty attitude, he wanted nothing more than to strip her naked and have his way with her right there in his office. Olivia was the exact opposite of every woman he dated, including Lindsay, and he couldn't pinpoint the reason he found her so attractive. They'd spent the next two weeks bickering and fighting like a couple of children. He'd threatened more than once to fire her, but Olivia had told him to shove it and got back to work. In the end, Olivia traced the man they were looking for quickly and efficiently, and the authorities had the man in custody within a few short hours. Olivia had thanked Selena for the opportunity to help with the case. Olivia had then subsequently refused every job Selena offered her through Jack. She even turned down a job offer to come work for Powell Trading, which would have resulted in higher pay and steadier work hours.

Ellis found himself watching Olivia for the next half hour, all thoughts of leaving having fled. She didn't seem to be enjoying herself, and she didn't stay in one place long. She seemed impatient to leave, much as he had been before he saw her across the room. She didn't appear to be with a date, and she didn't engage any of the partygoers in conversation. When she did finally stop to talk to someone, he saw it was Lindsay's best friend Mandy. Mandy had been a constant fixture in Lindsay's life. She had also been one of the two reasons his relationship with Lindsay fell apart. The first, and main reason, had been Lindsay's brother, Baxter. Baxter had hated Ellis on sight and had put a wedge between them. Ellis had gotten tired of Lindsay's devotion to her brother, who spent most of his time in a wheelchair, though he could walk. Baxter was hardly an invalid, and Ellis had finally gotten tired of her brother's negative attitude. Ellis had told her to choose. She'd chosen her brother.

Not that he blamed her. It hadn't been fair to make her choose, but Ellis had had enough. Then Mandy had swept in after the breakup and made an already bad situation worse. Mandy had tried to smear his reputation and destroy his career. Thankfully he met Jack shortly after the breakup, and Jack hadn't cared about the gossip surrounding him. Ellis was one of the best hackers in the country, and Jack knew a good thing when he saw it. He'd hired him immediately. A few years later, he'd ended up employed by Selena Powell as her bodyguard and security expert.

Ellis realized he was staring when Olivia raised her eyebrow at him. He'd been so absorbed in his thoughts that he hadn't realized she had stopped circling the room and was now watching him watch her. He pulled his gaze from hers, but he could still feel her watching him. He swallowed the last of his champagne and told himself he'd spent enough time at the reception to fulfill whatever weird obligation he had to Lindsay.

"Let me help." Olivia stood in front of Ellis, extending her arm to him. She saw his dark eyes once again find hers. Those eyes, Olivia thought, were enough to make any woman swoon. His looks weren't too bad either. He stood six-one to her five-six. His hair was pitch black and kept a little long on top but short on the sides, where hers was blonde and long. His eyes were dark brown pools, whereas her eyes were bright blue like a summer sky. His skin was dark olive, while hers was just lightly tanned. Two people couldn't be more different. And she had never been so drawn to a man as she was Ellis. He was exactly what she didn't want in a man. He was rich. He was classically handsome. He was incredibly smart. But buried beneath his polished good looks was a hard edge he couldn't quite conceal. If he chose to, he could easily overpower her, or any woman he wanted.

What frightened her the most was that she wasn't really frightened of him. They'd spent hours confined in his office, but not once had he made a move on her. Most men, when confronted with her prickly personality, tried to find the soft woman beneath the prickly exterior. Those men failed, of course, because they didn't want to know the real Olivia. They wanted to prove they were man enough to tame her. When their charm didn't work, most men resorted to name-calling, or worse, trying to force her into submission. Ellis hadn't done that. He'd fought with her, argued with her, but he hadn't called her names, and he hadn't tried to force himself on her. He didn't know it, but just the fact that he'd given as good as he got, without resorting to brute force, had gone a long way toward softening her attitude toward him.

So here she was, extending her arm to him to help him up. She knew he'd been shot. It had made the papers and the local news. But even if it hadn't, she would have known. Because Olivia's employer, Jack, was good friends with Selena Powell, she would have heard about it at work anyway. Jack knew why she had turned down several job offers from Ms. Powell. Olivia couldn't go back and work with Ellis again. He set off every feminine alarm bell she had ringing.

But despite the warning bells, her first inclination when she heard about the shooting had been to rush to his side. Knowing he wouldn't appreciate the gesture, she stayed away. Instead, she had kept track of his progress via her computer. Though highly illegal, she'd accessed his medical records to make sure he would make a full recovery. What she'd read had reassured her. But when she'd seen him last month, she'd been anything but reassured. Ellis had lost a lot of weight since the shooting. She'd been acting as security at Ms. Powell's wedding, where Ellis had been a guest. Olivia could only be grateful she'd been there in an official capacity because she would have gone over to him that night. Her heart had ached at the dark circles under his eyes and the way his tuxedo hung on his frame.

So what did she do the first time she came in contact with him outside her work? She found herself offering him her arm as he scowled at her. And instead of digging down deep for some feminine charm, she found herself getting defensive again. "Come on, Ellis. I won't bite. And you look like a good breeze would knock you over."

Ellis was tempted to shove her arm away, but not only would that probably please her, it would also be stupid to turn her down. Despite the progress he'd made with his physical therapy, by the end of each day, he was worn out and tired. Grudgingly he took the offered arm. He felt her slide closer to him, bracing some of his weight against her.

Olivia felt her heart twist in her chest. Now that he was standing, she could see he still hadn't gained all the weight back he'd lost. It had only been a month since she had seen him last, but she supposed she had expected him to have made more progress in his recovery. She didn't know much about gunshot wounds, but she'd studied his medical files religiously. The doctor was recommending that a personal trainer and a nutritionist be sent to his home. He had refused both.

Ellis leaned on her a bit as they walked through the crowd. "I certainly didn't expect to see you here. These people are not exactly your kind."

Instead of being offended, Olivia nodded. "No, they are not my kind. And despite my earlier opinion of you, I don't think they're your kind either. Why are you here?"

Her comment about her earlier opinion caught his attention. "Are you saying you might be wrong about me?"

Olivia nodded. "In some ways, perhaps. But not all. I still think you're arrogant. And I still think you're a bully. But I'm beginning to wonder about the rest."

Ellis would have pushed away but didn't have the strength. "You mean there's more?"

Olivia nodded again but went back to her earlier question. "I wouldn't think you would come to Lindsay's wedding, considering your history. And her new husband is probably not thrilled that his wife's ex-fiancé is in attendance."

Ellis frowned at her. "And what would you know about my relationship with Lindsay?"

Olivia led him outside. She held her hand out to Ellis for him to hand her his valet ticket. When he obliged, she handed the ticket to the man waiting. "I know more than you think. I'll tell you on the drive."

"The drive where?" Ellis let go of Olivia's arm and leaned against the brick half-wall surrounding the front of the hotel.

"You're not in any shape to drive yourself. As I said, you look like a good breeze would knock you over."

Ellis scowled, but he didn't feel up to arguing with her. Instead, he took the opportunity to admire the graceful line of her neck and back, the nice curve of her backside, along with her leg exposed by the dress. Despite his exhaustion, he felt his body stirring to life. It was always that way when he was around Olivia. She ticked him off, but he still wanted her. He wanted to feel those claws of hers digging into his back. He wanted to feel her soften beneath him as he made love to her. He wanted to kiss her until she couldn't fight him, only surrender to him.

"I probably don't want to know what you're thinking about right now, do I?" Olivia took the car keys from the valet and opened the passenger door for him.

"Probably not." Ellis eased himself into the passenger seat of his car. When she climbed into the driver's seat and started the engine, his common sense kicked in. "Do you drive a stick?"

Olivia shifted the car into gear and pulled out of the parking lot. "For the sake of your car, you had better hope the answer to that is yes."

Ellis felt his lips kick up into what was almost a smile. As she drove through the city and beyond, she handled his sports car effortlessly. "So what do you know about my relationship with Lindsay?"

"Just about everything, I suppose. You dated for a couple of years, then ten years ago the two of you got engaged. Not long after, she ended the engagement. You two hooked up now and again until five years ago. Since then, you've had a steady stream of women in your life. None of them serious."

Ellis couldn't make out her features in the dim light of the car. "And how do you know all that?"

"I'm Mandy's half-sister, and she recently married Lindsay's brother, Baxter. Not to mention, they've been best friends since high school."

Ellis's curse was loud in the quiet confines of the car. "I knew there was a reason I didn't like you."

Olivia shrugged and tried to tamp down the hurt his words inflicted. "Yeah, Mandy feels the same way about you. But don't take it personally. Mandy hates everyone. Well, except for Lindsay."

Ellis was having a hard time believing Olivia was related to Mandy. "You didn't mention you were related to Mandy when you came to work for me."

"Of course not. She's hardly a good character reference. Besides, my reasons for disliking you have nothing to do with Mandy or Lindsay. You remind me of someone."

"And who is that? I'm guessing it's not someone you like." Ellis tried to understand the odd turn their conversation had taken.

"You would be right about that. You did remind me of someone I didn't like. But like I said, I'm reassessing."

"So what, now you want to be friends?" Ellis looked over at Olivia, who was glancing between him and the road.

"Let's just say getting shot makes you more human. Less intimidating."

"Great. Just what I was hoping."

Olivia smiled at that. "I think I actually missed your sarcasm. I think I missed you. Which is really odd, given our previous relationship was so adversarial."

"I think you've lost me again." Ellis adjusted the seat belt where it was digging into his chest in an uncomfortable spot.

"Don't worry about it. I don't think linear. It's why I'm a better hacker than you are."

Ellis took offense to that. "You are not better than I am."

"I would have to disagree with you on that. But like I said, I think differently. You're a very black and white kind of man. You take the straight path set out before you. I wander off course, color outside the lines, so to speak. It makes me better than you."

Ellis glanced out the window. They were outside the gates of Selena's estate. Even though he was no longer her bodyguard, he still lived on the grounds. He had offered to move, but Selena and her new husband, Carter, assured him that it wasn't necessary.

"I'm still bigger and stronger than you are." Ellis leaned over Olivia to punch in the key code for the gate.

"On that, we can agree. But right now, you're not exactly in fighting form. I hate to take advantage of a man when he's down." Olivia drove straight to the front door of the smaller house on the left.

"How do you know where I live?" It suddenly occurred to Ellis that he hadn't told her.

Olivia shrugged and pointed to the GPS that had guided her to his home. She really hadn't needed the GPS, as she had looked up his address when she'd heard he was shot. She had wanted to come and see him at the hospital. Then she had thought about visiting him at his home. Though security was tight around Selena, it hadn't taken Olivia that long to track her down. Everyone knew Ellis lived on the property with Selena. Rumors were they were lovers at one point, but somehow Olivia didn't believe that. She had seen Selena and Jack together, and if anyone was involved with someone, it was those two. But even that hadn't lasted long. Olivia didn't know Selena well, but she had seen in Selena's eyes the same reserve Olivia felt around the males of the species.

"So now what? You drove me home. How are you getting home?" Ellis tried to get out of the sports car by himself, but in the end, took Olivia's arm when she offered it to him again.

"I'm going to take your car. You don't need it.

Tomorrow is Sunday, and you should be resting."

"This car costs over a hundred grand. You are not taking it." Ellis's hand was trembling as he tried to fit the key in the lock of his door. He felt Olivia's fingers take it from him. He turned the alarm off and headed straight for the back of the house.

Olivia stood in the entryway, interested in the surroundings. The house was mostly white. There was not a lot of color, but the dark wood tones of the furniture contrasted nicely. There was a colorful area rug in the living area that brightened everything up. She didn't see a television, but a very expensive laptop sat on the coffee table. She slowly followed the path Ellis took, stopping to admire the white kitchen cabinets and the light brown granite counters. Again, not much color, but the overall effect wasn't cold.

She stopped outside what she thought was probably Ellis's bedroom door. "Are you okay?"

"Go away." Ellis's voice was faint.

Olivia bit her lip, then decided things couldn't get much more awkward between them. When she pushed the door open, Ellis's half-naked back was to her. He had discarded the tux jacket and was trying to get the shirt off. Trying to be clinical about it, she came around to stand in front of him.

"You just can't follow a simple order." Ellis moaned a bit as the muscles in his chest tightened as he tried to pull off the shirt. The end of the day was the worst.

Olivia stilled his arm. She carefully eased the shirt off.

She tried not to stare at his chest, but that was impossible. The three mostly healed bullet wounds were impossible to miss. The skin was pink and puckered where the tissue was still healing. She couldn't help but touch the spot on his upper chest. This one could have been the one to end his life.

Ellis tried not to savor the soft touch of Olivia's fingers on his chest. He had imagined her in his bedroom, but this was not the way the fantasy went. Suddenly angry, he grabbed her hand and crushed her fingers.

"You're hurting my hand." Olivia tugged her hand, and for a moment she was afraid he wasn't going to let go. Then suddenly she was free.

"Go home, Olivia. I don't need your help or your pity." Ellis's hands went to the fastening of his pants. He kicked off the trousers, leaving him in a pair of boxers, and slid under the covers.

"Oh, yeah, that's right. You're made of steel. Nothing can keep you down for long. Blah, blah. I get it. You don't need a woman taking care of you. You can take care of yourself."

"Nothing wrong with a woman taking care of me. I just prefer it to be one that doesn't annoy the crap out of me."

"Well, you're stuck with me. As far as I can see, all your fancy girlfriends are nowhere to be found." Olivia tugged the covers up to Ellis's chin. He had been fruitlessly struggling to cover himself with the blanket.

"Give me the phone, and I'll call one. Now get out."

"Suit yourself. But she'll probably be useless. Too afraid

she'll break a nail or something." Olivia left his room in a huff. She knew she fell short of the type of woman he was attracted to. She would need to grow a pair of double D boobs and dye her hair black to attract him. And she'd probably need to learn to speak with some kind of exotic accent.

Ticked off and hurt at the same time, Olivia shut the door behind her with a slam. She thought she might have heard him call her name, but decided she was hearing things. She jingled his car keys as she reset his alarm. She's seen him punch in the code, so she could get back in later if she needed to. She also saw him punch in the code to the gate. No one got in or out without a code or the electronic device attached to the dash of the car. He had installed some pretty slick security, then he'd upgraded it after he was shot, but with his car and access code, she'd have no problem returning. She slid into the driver's seat and shifted the car into gear. She gazed back at the huge mansion Selena and her husband occupied. The house could probably fit twenty of her apartments inside.

Olivia accessed the gate and headed home. She was glad she had a garage unit she rented along with her apartment. Ellis's car would be stripped and sold for parts in a hot minute if left on the street. Thankfully it was dark outside her garage space, and no one was likely to notice the crazy expensive car she was putting inside it. She didn't own a car at the moment but rented the garage space for when she did. Of course, by the time she had the money for a car, she should probably consider moving to a better neighborhood first. But one thing at a time.

Olivia secured the garage door and made her way to her apartment. She rented a ground-floor apartment that was accessible from outside the building. She closed the door behind her and leaned against it. All in all, it had been a crazy night. And despite her previous resolve to stay away from Ellis Wallace, she was now devising a way to spend more time with him. He frightened her and attracted her at the same time. A year ago, she had let her fear overwhelm her. But time had passed; she had worked hard to become a stronger woman, and now it was time to explore her attraction. She wasn't sure how that was going to work, or if it was going to work, but knowing he was shot and seeing firsthand the damage that had been done, Olivia wasn't sure she could simply walk away from him again.

Step one would be returning his car. Step two would be gaining his acceptance of her help. And step three would be seeing if she could learn to trust again. If she could do those three things, then perhaps she could take the first step in exploring the feelings she had for him, and maybe knock down some of the barriers she had put up to protect herself.

Chapter Two

The witch had taken his car. Ellis leaned against the kitchen counter, sipping his second cup of coffee. He recalled telling her she couldn't take his car. And he remembered throwing her out. He vaguely remembered lying in bed and her tugging the covers over his chest. It also didn't get past his notice that his alarm had been reset, and she'd gotten off the estate. He had forgotten last night that she possessed an incredible memory. Memorizing the digits he'd punched into the keypad last night would have been easy for her to do. And it shouldn't have gotten past his attention last night that she would have picked it up. She'd been right next to the pad as he'd leaned over her and punched it in. But he'd been so focused on climbing into his bed, he'd forgotten whom he was dealing with.

But instead of phoning the cops, or calling her boss, Ellis simply stared out the window, enjoying the bright morning sunshine. He wasn't worried she'd stolen his car. He fully expected her to make an appearance again at some point today. He just couldn't figure out what her angle was. They weren't friends; they weren't even coworkers. It had been his experience that women usually wanted something when they were doing you a favor. Certainly, the women he dated ultimately wanted something from him. Some wanted the prestige his position with Powell Trading could give them. Some of them were looking for a man to take care of them.

Some even used him to make old husbands or lovers jealous.

Ellis supposed it was only fair. He'd used them to push memories of Lindsay out of his head. And he'd used them to push away regrets of what might have been. Had he not been such a jerk ten years ago, he could have been a happily married man with a couple of kids.

But he couldn't figure out what Olivia wanted. She wasn't looking for an affair. She wasn't looking for a job. She wasn't looking for prestige. And he was pretty sure she wasn't looking for a man to take care of her. So what did that leave?

Ellis's musings were interrupted when he saw the security gate swing open and his Porsche came through. He had to admit she handled the car well. Not only was the car a stick, but it had a powerful motor. He'd taken it out to the racetrack with a friend and they'd maxed out the speedometer. His friend hadn't been able to handle the car, but Olivia drove it like she'd been born in the seat of a racecar.

He almost choked on his coffee when Olivia swung out of the driver's seat. He'd had plenty of women in that car. Women who wore evening gowns and thousands of dollars in jewels had ridden in that car. He'd seduced a few women in that car. Trust Olivia to drive up in his Porsche wearing sweatpants and a sweatshirt. The woman had no sense of style.

Curious just how far she was going to go, he purposefully didn't answer the knock on his door. Instead, he remained where he was in the kitchen. He heard her pound louder on the door a second time. After a moment, he heard the front door open, and he heard the alarm being disarmed. He could hear her footsteps as they headed toward the back of the house, toward his bedroom. He moved silently from the kitchen and up behind her. He had her locked against his body and immobilized before she even realized he was behind her.

Olivia shrieked and tried to struggle against the arms that held her. They felt like steel bands. Her head was twisted back so far that she could hardly breathe to scream. She tried to kick out at the man who held her, but she couldn't move.

"Perhaps you'll learn a valuable lesson," Ellis spoke the words directly in her ear. He could feel her heart pounding against his arms. Sensing her very real fear, he let her go, holding her arm so she wouldn't lose her balance.

Olivia spun around and backed away from him. She took a deep breath and glared at Ellis. "You bastard. What did you do that for?"

Ellis shrugged. "Teaching you a lesson. You have no business breaking into someone's home. You're liable to get hurt. If I had been a different kind of man, you could be dead right now."

Olivia felt her knees trembling, but she locked them so she wouldn't fall. "I was worried when you didn't answer. I just wanted to make sure you were okay."

Seeing real, residual fear in her eyes had him feeling like

the bastard she had called him. He swept her up into his arms and carried her to the kitchen. He was tempted to drop her on her butt in the chair but set her down carefully instead. "Coffee?"

Unsure of what had just happened, Olivia nodded. "Cream and sugar, please."

Ellis poured her a cup and set the cream and sugar in front of her. "Should I even ask what you're doing here this morning?"

She dumped a couple of teaspoons of sugar in and a little cream. "Returning your car."

Ellis folded his arms across his chest. "You mean the car I distinctly recall telling you that you couldn't take?"

"That's the one. Figured you might start to get nervous if I kept it any longer. I was tempted to take it out for a drive up the coast, but I wasn't sure how long your patience would hold out."

Ellis leaned against the counter, watching her. She looked extremely serious. "Just where did you take it?"

"Just home. Don't worry, I parked in a secure garage. I woke up early and couldn't get back to sleep. So I took it out for a quick ride. Couldn't help showing it off. It's not every day a girl gets to drive a car like that."

Ellis unfolded his arms and came over so that he loomed over her. "And it will be the last time, too. Next time I will call the cops."

Olivia was not about to let him intimidate her. "I promised that if I ever got my hands on it again, I would take

Mrs. Davis out for a drive."

"Your Mrs. Davis is going to have to live with the disappointment." Ellis picked up the cream and sugar and put them away.

"You're into charity, right? Always at The Heart's Way Foundation fundraisers?"

"I believe in charity when people need it. I'm not feeling so charitable that I'd give my car away."

Olivia smiled up at him. "How about giving a ride to a nice old lady? Mrs. Davis is ninety-two. It would be the thrill of her life."

Ellis wasn't sure if she was playing him or if she was being serious. He changed the subject. "So besides returning my car, why else are you here?"

"I thought we could do each other a favor."

"I don't need any favors from you. If I need a woman, I can get my own. But thanks."

"Have you always been a jerk, or did you perfect it over the years?" Olivia rose and followed him out of the kitchen. He'd left her sitting alone when he made that last remark.

"Something about you just brings it out in me. Other women wouldn't have dared to make off with my car." Ellis stood next to his front door.

"Right. They'd have been in bed with you, not driving home. I get it. You're a lady's man. A stud. Always a new woman on your arm, with a few to spare on the side."

"Now that we've finished discussing my sex life, you should go find someone else to harass." Ellis held the door open.

"I don't have a ride home, remember. And besides, as I said, we can do each other a favor. And I don't mean sex."

Ellis didn't close the door, but he also didn't make a move toward her to throw her out. "I'm not sure what other type of favor you could possibly offer me."

"Give me a second." Olivia rushed past him and out to his car. She opened the small trunk and pulled a couple of canvas bags out.

Ellis was tempted to slam the door in her face, but the look on her face stopped him. She was smiling at him, a rare occurrence to be sure. When they'd worked together last year, she'd scowled at him most of the time. When she wasn't scowling, she was ignoring him.

Olivia brushed past him for a second time and headed back to his kitchen. She heard Ellis following her. His bare feet made a faint slapping sound on the tile floor.

"All right, I'll bite. What favor can we possibly do for each other that doesn't involve you and me getting naked?"

"Don't be crass. We both know I'm not your type."

She had that right. But that didn't stop his body from leaping to attention when she was near. "And I'm not yours. So?"

"I wouldn't say you're not my type. I suppose every woman fantasizes about a tall, dark, and handsome man sweeping her off her feet. And you're rich, so that just makes the fantasy that much better. But I'm not in the market right now. I was thinking of something a little more basic."

"More basic than sex?" Ellis found himself intrigued despite himself. Olivia did keep a man on his toes, even when he wanted to give in to his more basic urges. Of course, he wasn't sure what he wanted to do more: pull her over his knee or make love to her.

"I heard you've been refusing a personal trainer. Not to poke holes in your masculinity, but you're wasting away. You've lost a lot of weight and could stand to gain a few pounds."

Ellis folded his arms across his chest again. "And how would you know that?"

Olivia shrugged. "You know Jack. He likes to talk. And his wife stops in a lot. She's worried about you."

Jack's wife Theo had made more than a few comments about his weight. Of course, between Selena, Theo, and their friend Isabelle, he had three women nagging him about his weight. Their husbands, Carter, Jack, and John, had also made a few comments. Carter told him it was natural to lose weight after having been shot. He also said that it was natural to be depressed and not sleep well at night. Carter had been shot in the line of duty as a police officer. Ellis might have been shot in the line of duty, but it had been while protecting his client. He supposed getting shot was the same, no matter why. It hurt unlike anything he'd ever experienced before, and it very nearly killed him.

"All right, Olivia. What do you want from me?"

Olivia pulled several food items from her bag. "I'll help you work out and get you back up to your normal weight. In turn, you'll help me be a better bodyguard."

"Excuse me?"

"I figure you're the best person to help me. I've been working behind a computer for years. It's time I stepped out from behind my screens. There's more money in it. And I need money."

"You're a good hacker. You could make a fortune behind your computer."

Olivia slowly shook her head. "I've tried applying for corporate jobs, but so far no one will hire me. I've been doing investigative work too long, but I don't have a license. I had an offer from a couple of government agencies, but they don't pay well, either. I figure I could get myself a rich client and stash some cash."

"So you figure you can find yourself a nice, rich client who will pay you to be their bodyguard and hacker?"

"Don't act so sanctimonious. It worked for you." Olivia gathered up the food and started putting it in Ellis's fridge.

"I'm over six feet and intimidating. You're five-six on a good day and couldn't intimidate a fly."

"I resent that. I can be intimidating. And you're going to help me."

"And just how do you suppose you're going to make me do that?" Ellis was tempted to pick her up one-handed just to show her his superior strength. "Or have you forgotten how quickly I subdued you when you broke into my house?"

"I didn't break into your house. I was checking on you." Olivia scowled at him.

"Semantics. The reality is you don't have what it takes. Go back to your desk, Olivia. It's where you belong."

Olivia folded her arms across her chest, mimicking his earlier stance. "If you don't help me, I'll find someone who will. But either way, I'm not going anywhere. You need a workout partner, and you need someone who knows what you should be eating. I've been studying nutrition, trying to bulk up. It's been working."

Ellis came over. He grabbed her arm and slid the oversized sleeve of her sweatshirt up her arm. Surprisingly her arms were quite firm. A year ago, her arms were those of a computer analyst. "You really have been working out."

Olivia pulled her arm from his grasp. "Do we have a deal?"

Ellis could see how serious she was, but there was no way he was helping her. "Look, I appreciate the offer of a workout partner. And I appreciate you offering to feed me. But I'm not going to help you. No matter what you want, you won't ever be big enough to be a successful bodyguard. You're more likely to get yourself hurt."

Olivia tried to hide her disappointment, but she had prepared herself for that very answer. "Fine. Where's your gym? I assume you have a home gym. We can work out for a while, then I'll fix lunch."

"I just said I won't help you."

Olivia came and poked him in the chest with her forefinger. "And I said I was going to help you, either way. Someone has to take you in hand. The quicker you get better, the quicker you can get rid of me. I'm persistent, and you know it."

Ellis led her to the room that held his exercise equipment. "I guess my question is, why do you care?"

"I don't know why. You're a womanizing jerk, and I don't like you. But for some reason, I care."

"And you're an uptight, argumentative..." Ellis broke off what he was going to say.

"You can say it." Olivia looked him straight in the eye.

"Little witch." Ellis finished his sentence.

"You're close, anyway, but that should have started with the letter 'b.' Do you want my help or not? And you might as well say yes. I already know how to get into your house. You could change the code, but we both know I could crack it."

He thought about reminding her that he was bigger than she was but figured he'd be wasting his breath. And if nothing else, just the thought of a nice home-cooked lunch was enough to relent and let her stay. Since he fired his nurse, he'd been eating his cooking, which was limited. And being so tired at the end of each day, he was apt to skip dinner in favor of his bed.

Olivia took his silence as a yes. "Good. What's first?"

"First, I go change."

Olivia watched as Ellis headed out. She took the opportunity to strip out of her sweats. She'd worn them over her workout clothes. She'd bought the fashionable leggings and a matching sports bra as an incentive to workout. She figured if she was going to work out, it should be in style. And when she had gone to the gym for the first time, she had realized the women there seemed to have an unspoken rule about attire. She'd asked the first friendly face she met where to shop for the right clothes.

Ellis strode back into the room, this time wearing a t-shirt and basketball shorts. He stopped halfway in the room when he saw Olivia stretching in what had to be the tightest fabric made by man.

"All set?" Olivia stretched out her arms and legs. She realized Ellis was staring. "What?"

"What are you wearing?" Ellis barely got the words out.

Olivia glanced down, half afraid she had spilled food or something on her clothes. But the black stretchy fabric was clean. "My workout clothes. Got a problem with that?"

Ellis heard the defensive words but couldn't talk. He felt like the cartoon dog who had to fold his tongue in half to get it back in his mouth. The leggings hugged every curve, and she had them in all the right places. And the cleavage spilling out the top of her bra wasn't helping matters. He wasn't sure he'd be able to work out in his current state. And he was sure he wasn't going to be able to get the vision of her body out of his mind once she was clothed and gone.

"Stretches first, then." Olivia pulled out her notebook. "I keep my routine logged. I figure that my routine should be easy enough for you to start with."

Somehow, Ellis got himself under control. He let Olivia walk him through her daily routine. He was sweating and hurting halfway through. It was humiliating how weak his body was. He dropped down onto the weight bench. "No more."

Olivia finished her reps with the small weights she'd chosen. "You did well. I didn't think you'd get this far."

Ellis cursed under his breath but didn't argue with her. "I need a shower. You can use the one down the hall."

Olivia followed Ellis out and went to the bath he pointed to. She quickly showered and got dressed in the change of clothes she'd brought. Her muscles were already feeling sore. She knew she'd been showing off a little. A man like Ellis would appreciate his woman fit and lean. And when she heard that thought floating around her head, she made a face at herself in the mirror. She had a feeling she was playing with fire but couldn't seem to find the willpower to stop. If she wasn't careful, she might find herself head over heels in love with a man who had a new girlfriend every month. She was pretty sure she'd never seen him with the same woman more than a couple of times.

She brushed out her damp hair and braided it. She packed up her exercise clothes and headed back toward the living room. Ellis was stretched out on the couch.

Ellis glanced up at her. "You promised me lunch."

She gave him a slight smile and set her bag down by the front door. "So I did. Shouldn't take long. You can rest while I fix it up."

Ellis knew he should keep his butt planted on the couch but found himself following her to the kitchen anyway.

She'd changed into a calf-length sundress with no sleeves. Other than an evening cocktail dress, he'd never seen her look casual and put together at the same time. Drawn to her, he followed and watched as she prepared lunch.

He enjoyed the meal. He was pretty sure she couldn't squeeze in any other healthy foods. There was salmon served chilled, a spinach salad tossed with a variety of greens, and whole grain pasta tossed with avocados and tomatoes, and just a little bit of cheese crumbled on top. Before he knew it, he had finished what she had put in front of him. It had been a while since he'd finished a meal.

Olivia cleaned up the kitchen, then turned to Ellis. She'd been aware of his eyes following her movements around his kitchen. "I suppose I should call a cab. What time do you want me to come over tomorrow? I can write you a grocery list."

"I'll drive you home. You don't have to come over tomorrow, and I don't need you to make me a grocery list."

"Keep up with that kind of talk and I'm liable to think you don't want me around." Olivia ignored his glare and headed for the bag she had left by the front door.

He snatched the phone she'd pulled out of her bag from her hand. "What are you doing? I said I'd drive you home."

"I heard that part, but I'm ignoring it. So that way when I show up tomorrow, I can pretend I didn't hear the rest of what you said."

"You want to explain to me again why you want to help me?" Ellis tossed her phone into her bag instead of handing it back to her. He picked up her bag, fetched his keys from where she had left them on the table by the door, and ushered her out of his house.

"When I figure out the answer to that question, I'll let you know. Can I drive?"

"No, you can't drive." Ellis held open the passenger door. He had to refrain from slamming it. He wasn't sure what was bothering him so much about her wanting to help him, but it did. He couldn't figure out her motive.

Olivia bit her lip as she watched him round the car. She wished she knew the answer to his question. Last year when they had worked together, she had been withdrawn or argumentative at every turn. She'd told herself he was just another womanizing jerk who liked to string women along. She'd heard her half-sister Mandy and Lindsay trash-talk him over the years. She supposed she'd picked up some preconceptions about him from them. But when she'd heard he'd been shot, something inside had ached for him. And since the shooting, she'd become a borderline stalker, though he didn't know it. And now she felt compelled to make sure he got healthy again.

"Address?" Ellis interrupted her thoughts. She had drifted off.

"Tomorrow is Monday, but I have the day off work. Tell you what, you tell me what time to come over tomorrow, and I'll give you my address."

"What kind of deal is that?" Ellis started the engine and headed toward the gate.

"If you don't tell me, then I'll spend the rest of the day in your car while you try to find where I live." Olivia folded her arms across her chest and tried to look confident.

"I told you before, I'm a better hacker than you. I can find your address in two minutes." Ellis drove out past the gate and verified that it was closed.

"Yeah, but you're not near a computer. Time?"

Ellis reluctantly gave in. "Ten. But you're not making a grocery list."

Olivia gave him a big smile and rattled off her address. "I can't promise to make you a meal every day if you don't go buy what I write down. I can't afford to feed a man your size."

Ellis glanced over at her. It hadn't occurred to him what the food she brought must have cost her. And he couldn't tell if she was being serious or facetious. But given the address she'd given him, he had a feeling she was serious.

"All right. Make your list and bring it. If you want to be my workout buddy, then fine. But I don't cook, and I am not going to help you practice being a bodyguard."

"Fine. Make a left at the next light." Olivia kept her eyes on the road.

Thirty minutes later, Ellis was pulling into the parking lot of her apartment building. "Please tell me you didn't leave my car parked out here last night."

Olivia shrugged. "I didn't leave your car parked out here last night."

Ellis cupped her chin. He hadn't liked the way she'd

parroted him. "Seriously?"

She jerked her chin from his grasp and pointed to the line of garages. "Seriously. I have a parking garage. When I moved here, I had a car. Given the neighborhood, I figured I'd better lock it up at night. But I had to scrap the car last year, so it's been empty. No one was out last night, so no one saw me park it. It was perfectly safe."

"I know Jack pays you well. Why do you live here?" Ellis asked while she opened the door.

Olivia leaned in. "Maybe one day I'll tell you why. See you tomorrow."

Ellis watched as she strolled across the parking lot and into her apartment. He pulled out and headed home. He wasn't sure what he'd gotten himself into, but for better or worse, he was going to be spending a lot of time with Olivia Knight.

Chapter Three

Olivia buzzed the front gate at five after ten. When she got to his front door, he opened it before she knocked. She gave him a bright smile when he let her in.

"I suppose it was too much to hope you wouldn't show up." Ellis closed the door behind her. She was wearing a pair of cargo shorts and a t-shirt. This time, she had a backpack slung over her shoulder.

"Yep, it was too much to hope. It sure is warm out there today." Olivia wiped a bit of sweat from her brow.

Ellis looked past her and realized there was no car. Then he remembered her saying she had scrapped it. "How did you get here?"

"There's a bus that dropped me off about a mile down the road. I walked from there. So I'm all warmed up and ready to work out."

Ellis scowled at her retreating back. "You took a bus and walked? Does that mean I won't have to tolerate your company on rainy days?"

Olivia tossed her backpack down. "You want to be surly? Fine. I can be surly, too. But it would pack more punch if my muscles weren't bigger than yours."

Ellis watched as she pulled her workout clothes from her bag and headed to his bathroom. He knew exactly why he was acting surly today. He'd spent the better part of the day after he'd dropped her off thinking about her. Then he lay in his bed last night, half aroused, remembering the snug fit of her leggings. He had hoped, fervently hoped, she would not show up, though he hadn't believed she would stay away. Now he was just tired and crabby, and still a little aroused.

Olivia came back into the room. "I thought we could just do some yoga today. After the workout yesterday, I'm feeling a little stiff."

"I don't do yoga."

"What, are you too manly for it, or something? It will help with your posture and strengthen your muscles. The weights are fine and dandy, but with that wound on your chest, it must hurt. I also brought my bands. Some resistance training instead of your weights might be a good place to start, too."

Ellis submitted to most of the exercises she had for him. He refused most of the yoga, but he did use her bands. When he used his free weights or his weight machine, he quickly became frustrated when he couldn't lift what he used to and couldn't do as many reps as he used to. The bands offered enough resistance to be a challenge, but not so much that he couldn't use them for longer periods of time.

After an hour, they did a few cool down exercises. Olivia handed Ellis a bottle of water and took a few large gulps of her own.

"I brought something for you." Olivia rose from the bench where she had taken a seat and headed for her backpack.

"Let me guess, the grocery list." Ellis emptied the bottle.

"I have that, too. Take off your shirt." Olivia turned back to him with a small bottle in her hands.

"Why stop there?" Ellis stripped his shirt off. It wasn't as impressive as it used to be, but he still thought it wasn't half bad.

"I do love your sarcasm." Olivia poured some of the contents from the bottle into her palm. She recapped it, then emulsified the liquid in her hands.

Ellis sat still, slightly bemused when she started rubbing her hands on his chest where the wound was. The strong scent of menthol and wintergreen burned his nostrils. "I have stuff that doesn't smell so bad in the bathroom cabinet."

Olivia ignored him, but she couldn't quite ignore his chest. Despite his weight loss, there was still strength in his body. And his chest was quite impressive. Not to mention it had been a long time since she'd touched a man's chest with this degree of intimacy. The last man's chest she touched had been as a caregiver. And even though she was touching him as a caregiver, she wanted to touch him as a lover.

Ellis let her finish massaging the oil into his skin. He could feel the heat of her touch through the warmth of the oil. When she would have pulled her hands away, he covered them with his own. When she looked up at him, for the first time in her eyes, he saw desire there. So he did what any other man would do.

Olivia bit back her cry of surprise as Ellis took her mouth with his. His hands held hers firmly to his chest as his mouth seduced hers. She supposed she'd known he'd be a great kisser. His lips were firm, and the pressure of his mouth was exactly what she'd been craving. With her hands on his chest, she could feel his increased heart rate, and one nipple hardened under her palm.

Ellis released her hands, cupping her under her arms to lift her into a standing position, not breaking contact with her mouth. Her taste was sweet where he expected sour. Her hands were trembling where he expected steady. When he probed her lips to see if she would open them, she wrapped her arms around his neck and let him take what he sought.

Olivia lost herself in the kiss. Part of her mind tried to remember if any man had ever kissed her like this, and she was certain the answer was no. There was no hesitation in Ellis's kiss. There was no uncertainty or nerves. What she felt from him was desire, and she wanted to return it; oh, how she really did. But reality started to reassert itself, and she pulled away.

They were both breathing heavily when they separated. She didn't try to play coy or act like the kiss was no big deal. That was the most intense kiss she'd ever experienced in her life. And because she wanted more, she took a step back. She let out a breath when he let her go.

Ellis grabbed a towel off the rack and tossed her one. "That got a bit out of hand. Only inevitable, I suppose."

Olivia caught the towel, but she didn't understand what he meant. "What was inevitable?"

"Mmm. The kiss. Can't blame a guy for being curious."

Ellis tossed the towel in the nearby hamper.

Olivia figured she had two responses. She could act hurt, which is how she felt; or she could simply agree and move on. She chose the latter option. "Or a lady, I suppose. You kiss nice. But then you've had a lot of practice. Let me get the grocery list from my bag. These days you can get anything delivered, so I figured you could just place an online order and get it dropped off. Today you'll have to be on your own. I have a bus to catch, and I don't want to miss it. Tomorrow I can fix something healthy if you place that order."

"I'll drive you home." Ellis heard the offer come out of his mouth, and surprisingly, he meant it. He wasn't ready for their time to end.

"Not necessary. I took the bus in; I can take it out. I'd take a shower first, but I'm just going to get hot and sweaty walking. I'll see you tomorrow."

Ellis shook his head as she headed for the door. "Not tomorrow. I won't be here."

"That's right, you have a doctor's appointment. That will give you an extra day to get groceries. I'll see you the day after that." Olivia opened the front door and was a bit shocked when Ellis shoved it closed.

"How do you know I have a doctor's appointment tomorrow? I didn't tell you." Ellis leaned against the door, blocking her way out.

Olivia closed her eyes and called herself a fool. She knew he had an appointment because she had his files flagged on her laptop. She tried to brazen it out. "You must have told me yesterday on the way home."

"Has anyone ever told you that you're a terrible liar? You have to learn to be able to look someone in the eye when you lie to them. How did you know?" Ellis crossed his arms across his chest, prepared to stand there all day if he had to.

"All right, all right. I sort of poked into your medical records. I wanted to make sure you were all right. You were so pale at Selena's wedding, and you didn't look any better at Lindsay's." Olivia looked him in the eye.

Ellis thought about being mad about it, but she looked sincere. And she had looked worried the night she'd driven him home. In a weird way, he was flattered. She didn't like him, but she had worried about him. Instead of getting angry, he took her in his arms and gave her a rough kiss.

Olivia didn't get a chance to kiss him back. He released her as quickly as he had grabbed her. Her lips were still swollen from his earlier kiss, and this one made her lips tingle. "I should go."

"I'll drive you." Not taking no for an answer, he grabbed his keys and took her to the car. The ride was silent.

Olivia quickly got out of the car when they arrived at her apartment complex. "I'll see you the day after tomorrow."

Ellis nodded and waited until she was safely indoors.

* * *

They fell into a routine of sorts. Olivia took the bus and

walked to his house after work. They would work out for an hour or so. Then they'd have dinner. He started driving her home after each workout, not wanting her to be on the bus late in the evenings. He was also having a hard time getting their kiss out of his head.

Tonight she was making some kind of rice dish. It looked fancy, and it smelled amazing. She was a fantastic cook. In the two weeks they had been working out, he had already gained a few pounds. He was getting stronger, though his chest still ached. He kept the bottle of oil she'd brought over for him, but he put it on himself. If she put her hands on him again, he couldn't promise not to return the favor.

But in addition to lust, he wanted to know more about her. She came over every day. Some days she was pleasant company, and other days they would argue. Sometimes he liked to provoke her, just to watch her temper flare. However, tonight he wasn't interested in arguing. He wanted some answers.

"So, why do you live in that apartment? You told me you'd tell me one day." Ellis took a pull from his bottle of beer. He'd been surprised when she had asked if she could have one. All the women he dated drank fancy wines or fancier drinks.

Olivia chopped the rest of the veggies and slid them into the pan. She wished she had a wok, but Ellis's kitchen didn't run beyond the basics. She kept her back to him but felt it was time she told him. Since the morning of their kiss, she'd thought of little else. And if she wanted their relationship to go beyond their tentative friendship, she needed to be open and honest with him.

"My husband left me a lot of debt. I've been paying it off little by little. I moved out of the apartment we lived in when he died. I couldn't afford it on my own."

Ellis choked on his beer. "Husband?"

Olivia turned the heat down. She took a drink of her beer before she faced him. "Yes, husband. I was married for five years. He died of pancreatic cancer. It's incurable. He got lots of very expensive treatments, but they couldn't keep him alive. He was a fighter; I'll give him that."

"You sound bitter. How long ago did he die?"

Olivia took a deep breath and let it out slowly. She still got angry when she thought about her husband. "Dennis died about six months before I met you. Let's just say I was still feeling raw when we met. It wasn't a good marriage, and I was in the process of dissolving it when he got sick. It didn't seem right to divorce a dying man. So I played the dutiful wife until the end."

Ellis crossed the room and took her hand. He unfolded the fingers she had dug into her palms. He soothed away the nail marks. "I think there's a bit more to the story."

Olivia looked down at the hand that held hers. "There is. Dennis married me because he liked my father. I married him because I thought he would make a good husband, and I desperately wanted someone in my life. It sounds pathetic now, but that was how it was. He cheated on me within the first year of our marriage. He apologized, swore it wouldn't happen again, and I was too afraid to be alone, so I believed him. I think he was faithful for a while. Then he started cheating again but had gotten better at hiding it. It wasn't until our fourth anniversary that I woke up and realized what he was doing. I told him I wanted a divorce."

"And then he told you he had cancer." Ellis stepped past her and stirred the veggies in the pan.

Olivia nodded. "I had hired a lawyer and moved out. I took half our bank account and transferred it into my own. Then Dennis came to the apartment I was renting a couple of weeks before the papers were to be final. It had taken almost a year to come to an agreement. I was strapped for cash because of all the lawyer's fees. Dennis was fighting me for everything. Just the week before, I had gotten the job with Jack and was finally standing on my own two feet. Dennis first asked me to drop the divorce. I told him no. Then he told me he had cancer. For the first time in our marriage, he looked scared and unsure."

"And you were still his wife, so you dropped the divorce proceedings and took care of him."

Olivia couldn't tell from his face or his tone what he thought. "I felt bad for him. He was genuinely scared, and he needed me. He had no other family besides me. His girlfriend wasn't sticking by his side. She bailed on him. So he came to me, and I went back. He lived nine months, and those were the toughest nine months of my life. I cared about him and hated him at the same time. Toward the end, he was incredibly mean. He would say the most horrible things to me. Told me I was a lousy wife. Told me I was a lousy lover. He told me in detail what the other women he slept with gave him that I couldn't. Then he died."

Ellis took the pan off the stove. Then he pulled Olivia into his arms. "Not many women would have stayed by his side, especially after what he'd done."

Olivia leaned up against him. "I was his wife. I couldn't desert him. But his medical bills were astronomical. I found out he had cashed out his insurance money and he had cashed out his pension the year before. The entire time we were separated, he was living it up with the woman of the day. A fact he threw in my face often. By the time he died, there was nothing left, and the debt was beyond belief. Some of it was written off to charity, and the rest was mine to pay."

"Like I said, not many women would have stayed by his side. You must have still been feeling raw when we met."

Olivia pulled back enough to meet his eyes. "I was very raw. I was angry, mostly. I ended up seeing a therapist because I didn't know how to vent my anger, or where to direct it. But you were exactly the opposite type of man I wanted to be attracted to. You were rich, handsome, and had women falling all over you. I had heard enough gossip from my half-sister about you. She liked to remind Lindsay that she was better off without you. I chalked you up as another Dennis, a man who doesn't know how to be faithful. I was wrong."

"So the attitude was because you were attracted to me?" Ellis settled his hands on her shoulders.

She tried to shrug them off. "I know it was stupid. When Dennis died, I felt like he took a part of me with him. The soft, vulnerable side that cared about others. When I heard you'd been shot, I felt compassion and caring for the first time in ages. I thought that if I spent time with you, maybe you could help me get that part of myself back. I thought maybe if I could learn to trust you, things might be different, that I could see where this attraction I feel for you could go."

Ellis let her go, but he didn't turn his back on her. She had bared a piece of her soul to him, but he didn't know what to do with it. Perhaps he could give her a piece of his. "When Lindsay broke off our engagement, I felt she had taken a part of me with her, too. She was the first and only woman I've ever loved. And in the end, she broke my heart. I tried to put the pieces back together, and when that didn't work, I tried to get her back. We played at being lovers on and off for five years after she ended our engagement. In the end, we couldn't make it work."

Ellis took a deep breath. "But perhaps you're right about trust. I didn't, and don't, trust the women I date. I spent years trying to be in love with Lindsay and failed. You weren't that far off the mark when you called me a womanizer. There have been a lot of them since Lindsay. But they weren't looking for a serious commitment any more than I was. We had fun. But it never went beyond that. But I never cheated. There was only ever one at a time."

Olivia had to ask the question poised on her lips. "And if

you found a woman you could trust, do you think you could love her the way you loved Lindsay?"

Ellis gave her a sad smile. "I like to think that if I found a woman I could trust, I could love her better than I did Lindsay. My love for her was selfish. I asked her to choose between me and her brother. She chose her brother, and rightly so. So, no, I couldn't, nor would I want to love another woman the way I loved Lindsay."

Olivia digested that bit of information and held it close to her heart. "You're not like any other man I know, except maybe Jack. You can be brutally honest, but you aren't mean. You can be surly, argumentative, and annoying, but you still aren't mean."

"Are you saying I'm a wimp?" Ellis wasn't sure how to take her statement.

Olivia stood up on her tiptoes and lightly kissed Ellis on the mouth. "No, I'm saying you're a nice man, and I didn't think you would be."

"I'm not sure too many men want to be categorized as nice. But I'll let that slide for now if you feed me what you've got in the works."

Olivia guessed the time for serious talk was over. She'd told him about her husband and why she'd behaved the way she had when they'd met. She thought she'd taken a good first step toward trust. And maybe they'd made a good first step toward a real friendship.

Olivia finished making their dinner, and she was pleased when Ellis ate a second helping. He was on the mend. It made her heart happy to see him getting better, and a bit sad because he wouldn't need her help much longer. In a week or so, he would start going back to work, and their workouts together would end.

Olivia took the last bite of her dinner. She would just have to find another reason to hang out with Ellis. If she learned nothing else tonight during their heart-to-heart, it was that she wanted more. She wasn't sure how much more, but she had a feeling she wanted everything he had to give. And she wanted to give him everything she had.

While she finished washing up the dishes and Ellis grabbed his keys to drive her home, she realized she had gone and done what she had feared she'd do. She'd fallen in love with Ellis Wallace.

Chapter Four

"Are you going to tell me what's going on between you and Olivia Knight?" Selena sat next to Ellis on his sofa, the two of them going over some of the work Ellis was missing out on while he recovered. Selena had popped in a few times a week once she was back from her honeymoon to check up on him and came over once a week for work.

Ellis couldn't help but smile a bit at the thought of Olivia. "I am not sure exactly what is going on. She's helping me work out and cooking for me."

"Sounds like you're dating her." Selena set her computer aside and focused on Ellis. Selena liked Olivia; the woman had spunk, and Selena still wished she'd taken her up on her job offer.

"Not hardly. As I said, she's helping me out, whether I like it or not."

"Since she's been coming around for a few weeks now, I'd say you're not trying very hard to get rid of her."

Ellis grunted at that. "No, I don't suppose I am. And to give her credit, she has helped me put on a few pounds."

Selena looked him over. "Yes, she has. They look good on you. So have you kissed her?"

"What kind of question is that?" Ellis was surprised by her questions. Selena wasn't one to pry into his personal life.

"I take it that's a yes. Slept with her yet?"

Now that almost shocked him. "No, I have not. And even

if I did, that is not the type of question you should be asking me."

Selena chuckled. "I asked Carter if he thought something was going on between you two, and he told me to ask you. Said he wouldn't speculate."

"That's because Carter knows it's none of his business."

Selena's words took on a serious tone. "I've been worried about you. You haven't had a single date since you were shot. You spend a lot of time cooped up here. You aren't even working. And then you went to Lindsay's wedding, which really had me concerned. I guess I had hoped Olivia could get you completely back to normal."

"Dating Olivia would not get me back to normal. She's liable to drive me mad. She's not anything like the woman I date. And sex isn't going to fix my problems."

Selena blushed. "It has recently solved a lot of mine. I just want you to be happy."

Ellis made a face at her. "That's just not right. We are not going to talk about your sex life, any more than we're going to talk about mine. At least not to each other."

Selena leaned over and kissed Ellis's cheek. "Okay, I'll back off. I suppose it is like talking to a brother. But don't discount her. I think she'd be good for you; keep you on your toes."

Ellis was saved from responding to that question when the buzzer from the gate rang. "That will be her. I haven't told her I'm going back to work tomorrow. You might want to take off. It might not go well."

Selena packed up her work bag and watched Ellis as he opened the front door and waited for Olivia to walk up the drive. She couldn't help the pleased smile. Ellis talked like he wasn't interested, but he was.

"Sorry, I'm late. I got held up at work, and then the bus ran late." Olivia came through the front door, chatting until she saw Selena.

"I'm just on my way out." Selena brushed past the pair and out the front door. She waved at them as she made her way up the path to her house.

Olivia gave her a slight smile and waved back, but she was happy to see Selena go. Her time with Ellis was running out, and she didn't want to share her time.

"Working hard?" Olivia carried her bag back to Ellis's workout room.

"She's finally settled back in after having been away on her honeymoon. I was catching up on some last-minute details. My first day as her new vice president is tomorrow."

That stopped Olivia in her tracks. She'd known he was stronger than he'd been a few weeks ago. She knew he didn't need her help anymore, but these past few weeks had been great. It was nice working out with a friend. She supposed she could still come over when he got home from work, but somehow, she had a feeling that in his mind, going back to work was proof he didn't need anyone's help anymore. Especially hers.

"You must be excited. I take it your doctor has released you to go back to work."

Ellis remained in the doorway to his gym. "Given the fact that you've been spying on me, medically speaking, you know he did. I'm to keep up the exercise, but not overdo it. And I'm supposed to keep up with healthy eating habits. He figures that within the next couple of months I'll be back to normal, or as much as one can be after having been shot."

"Just keep buying the foods I've been fixing for you, and you'll be fine. I've no doubt you'll keep working out until you've gotten all your strength back."

"Guess you'll have to find someone else to harass." Ellis tried to make a joke of it, but it fell flat.

Olivia turned her back on him without responding. She instead focused on her stretches.

Ellis came up behind her. "Look, I appreciate what you've done for me. I do owe you one."

Olivia looked up at him. "I've been thinking of a way you can repay me."

"If this is about helping you train to be a bodyguard, we've been through this." Ellis dropped onto the weight bench. He'd already worked out that morning.

Olivia dropped onto the mat, sitting lotus-style, giving up on her stretches. She had no desire to work out tonight, and it looked as if Ellis was not planning to join her. "Actually, I need a date. I thought maybe you could be it."

That threw him for a loop. "What do you need a date for?"

Olivia shrugged. "It's just a birthday party, but it's going to be at a nice restaurant. Several of the people attending will be bringing a date. It would be nice to have one instead of going solo. And it will get my friends off my back about not stepping back into the dating pool."

It was a simple thing she was asking him to do, but he hesitated.

Olivia stood up when he didn't respond. "Forget it. You don't owe me anything. I did what I did because I wanted to, not because I expected to be repaid. If you can't stand the thought of spending one more evening with me, then don't."

Ellis blocked the door when she would have pushed past him. "All right. I'll take you to your birthday party. It might get Selena off my back about dating, too."

Olivia nodded but couldn't find any enthusiasm in his acceptance. "Well, then. Since it doesn't seem like we're going to work out tonight, let's get dinner done and over with."

Ellis halted her. "I already worked out, and I already ate with Selena. Her husband is working late tonight, and she didn't want to eat alone."

"Then you should have called me and told me not to come." This time, Olivia did make her way past him.

"Believe it or not, I wanted to see you. I wanted to tell you in person that I was going back to work and that I appreciate all of your help."

Olivia went back and picked up her bag. "Please take me home. I am happy you're healthy again. And you're welcome."

Ellis wasn't sure what else to say. She walked out his

front door toward his car. He followed her out and hit the button to unlock the doors. The drive was done in silence. He would have preferred her sarcasm to the silent treatment, but he had known the night would end this way.

Olivia took a deep breath and finally spoke when he pulled up in front of her apartment building. "The party is on Saturday. I'll text you the time and place. We can meet up there."

"A proper date would be me picking you up."

"Since it's a pretend date, with both of us attending to get people off our backs about dating, there's no need. And I'll be at the restaurant early decorating. See you then, if you can make it."

Olivia hurried into her apartment and opened the curtain to see Ellis pull away. She felt tears sting her eyes. She blinked them away. She closed the curtain and went to her bedroom. She stripped and climbed into bed, even though it was still early. She wasn't hungry, and she was feeling too depressed to do any of the normal things she would do on a quiet night after work.

She supposed she had no right to be angry with Ellis. He hadn't wanted her help in the first place. They'd shared an incredible kiss, and they'd shared a piece of themselves. But Olivia hadn't been prepared for the vulnerability Ellis made her feel. And she didn't like the ache she felt in her chest. Yes, she would see him again for the party. She wasn't worried he would stand her up. He felt obligated to her, so he would do his duty. But Olivia didn't want obligation.

Olivia punched her pillow and rolled on her side. The problem was she wasn't sure what she wanted. When she met him, she couldn't stand him. Then something shifted inside her when he'd been shot. Now here she was, in love with a man who was everything she didn't want, and her heart was breaking because he didn't feel the way she did. It was pathetic really. And the worst part was that she was too much of a coward to tell him how she felt, or even tell him that she wanted to spend more time with him. Dating seemed like a nice, safe place to go from work out buddies to friends. And dating could take them from friendship to something more.

Olivia gave a half laugh and punched her pillow again. She was assuming he would even want to date her, much less take a friendship with her to something more. He was handsome. He was rich. He was intelligent. And he had dozens of women who met his physical needs and desires. Olivia was just the annoying California blonde computer analyst who had forced herself on him. She had no doubt he'd show up for her party. And she had no doubt he'd take one look at her friends, think she was pathetic, take her home, and never see her again.

Olivia wiped away her unwanted tears and forced herself to sleep. Saturday night would come soon enough, and the fantasy she'd been weaving between her and Ellis would die a slow death.

* * *

"Depression doesn't look good on you, my dear." Mrs. Davis patted Olivia's hand. She had finally gotten Olivia to sit for a minute. The girl had been running around like a madwoman for the past two days, making sure everything was perfect for the birthday party.

Olivia glanced away from the sharp gaze of the older woman. "I don't suppose it looks good on anyone. But I think I've rather gotten the hang of it."

"You're too young to be so sad. And your man is still coming tonight, isn't he?"

"He will be here. He sent me a text earlier that he might be running a little late. He just went back to work, and he said he's been tied up all week." Olivia fussed with the floral arrangement on the table.

"That's good then. Maybe he can get that gloomy look off your face."

"He's the reason I have this gloomy look on my face. After tonight's party, I doubt I'll see him again. He's only coming because he thinks he owes me."

"I'm sure it's more than that." Mrs. Davis stilled Olivia's hand.

"I know what being an obligation feels like. I've been one my whole life. I should never have asked him. And I should grow a spine and stop whining." Olivia stood up. She straightened her skirt and took a final look around the room.

"You're entitled to whine a bit now and again. I used to

drive my husband crazy sometimes when I got in a mood. He'd do whatever he could to get me out of it. He was pretty good at it, too. You've been through a lot in your life, and you deserve a bit of happiness."

Olivia turned to look at Mrs. Davis. "Maybe. But I'm not sure Ellis will make me happy. I think he's more apt to make me crazy."

Mrs. Davis gave her a huge grin. "Crazy is better in some ways. My Jonathan drove me crazy at times, but it was a good crazy. And when he wasn't driving me crazy, he made me very happy."

Olivia sighed. "I don't think they make them like they used to. Men, I mean."

"I wouldn't be too sure about that. Your first marriage ended badly. But you've had time to grieve. You're young and resilient. And you're determined. You go after what you want. And if you want your man, you'll do what you have to do to get and keep him."

Olivia couldn't help but smile at that. She had a vision of her chasing Ellis until he was too tired to run from her anymore. He'd beg for mercy, and she'd grant it to him, but only after he promised to love and cherish her. It was a nice fantasy, but she had a feeling Ellis could outrun her.

Once Mrs. Davis's friends arrived, the party got underway. Olivia was the youngest person in the room. Mrs. Marnell was 87 and had been Mrs. Davis's best friend for over fifty years. Mrs. Hornsby was 92, the same age as Mrs. Davis. Her husband was still alive but was at home, supposedly watching a ball game. Mrs. Hornsby said he was most likely sound asleep in the recliner. It was rare for her husband to leave the comfort of his chair and the blasting sound of his television.

There were several other attendees, people Mrs. Davis had met over the years. People from her senior group rarely missed a free meal, so several of them were in attendance. There were a few people from her apartment building, a complex for seniors, there was well. Olivia had met Mrs. Davis on the bus. The route that took Olivia to work each day took Mrs. Davis to her doctor's appointments. Mrs. Davis had engaged her in conversation one day, and the rest was history. Olivia enjoyed the time she spent with the older woman, though her work kept her from spending as much time with her as she'd like. Over the past year, she'd gotten to know her friends, too.

The party was about half an hour underway when she saw Ellis enter the private room. It only took a moment for his eyes to find her. She watched him give her a once-over, then watched as his attention wandered around the room. If he was at all dismayed to see the over-eighty crowd enjoying the party, he didn't give a hint of it away on his face.

Olivia crossed the room to greet him. "I'm glad you could make it. Let me introduce you."

Ellis shrugged out of his jacket. "Sorry, I'm late. I had a call that ran over."

"It's ok. The ladies will keep the party going until they get kicked out. They don't get together that often, at least not on a scale of this size."

"So who's birthday?" Ellis looked around again. He was pretty sure he and Olivia were the only people under seventy at this party.

Olivia took his arm in hers. "It's Mrs. Davis's ninety-second birthday."

"The woman you want to take for a drive in my car?" Ellis smiled and greeted people as they made their way through the crowd.

Olivia looked up at him in surprise. "Yes. She's the one. I told her you were coming tonight, and she's anxious to meet you."

Ellis allowed himself to be taken to the woman who sat in the place of honor at the party. Though he couldn't say she didn't look her age, he would have guessed her to be in her early eighties, not the ninety-two she was. Her weathered face sported a huge smile.

"He sure is a handsome devil. It's wonderful to meet you." Mrs. Davis slowly got to her feet to shake the man's hand who had found his way into Olivia's battered heart. She figured he must be something quite special to have done so.

"My pleasure. I'm honored to be invited to such a milestone in your life."

"And a charmer." Mrs. Davis sat back down, not wanting to admit how badly her knees ached tonight.

Olivia took his jacket and hung it on a nearby chair. "He is that. Dinner should be served soon. I'm sitting here."

Ellis took a seat at the table across from Mrs. Davis. He had a feeling he was about to be grilled.

"So, young man, what do you do?"

"I'm the vice president of Powell Trading. I was previously the head of security."

Mrs. Davis frowned. "Oh, my. You aren't the man who was shot, are you? I remember the news reports about Ms. Powell having been attacked and saved by her security team."

Ellis took a sip of water. The ache in his chest muscles reminded him often of what had happened. "Unfortunately, yes, I am. A gunman shot at Ms. Powell. It was my job to stop him. There was another man on her security team who took the gunman out. She recently married him."

Olivia shuddered and took a sip of her wine. Though she knew the details of the shooting, it was difficult to hear them from his lips. "He's extremely lucky to be alive."

"Indeed. So now you're the vice president. Getting shot seems an extreme way to get promoted." Mrs. Davis's eyes twinkled a bit.

Ellis chuckled. "I wouldn't recommend it. But I will admit I think I'm going to enjoy being behind a desk, at least for a while."

"I imagine you're more of a man of action. But I believe you'll live up to the challenge. And if you keep seeing our lovely Olivia, she'll be enough to keep you on your toes."

Olivia choked a bit on her wine at the tone in Mrs. Davis's voice and her obvious matchmaking.

"Of that, I have no doubt." Ellis lifted his glass in a slight toast to Olivia.

For the rest of the evening, Ellis charmed her friends. Olivia was amazed when he even got the perpetually grumpy Mrs. Markle to laugh.

It was close to ten when the party started winding down. Most of the group had money for a cab. Olivia went to Ellis as he was gathering his coat. "I'm glad you came tonight."

Ellis pulled on his jacket but didn't button it. "I had a nice time. Though I wish we had more time to chat."

Olivia let Ellis help her with her jacket. "I didn't think the ladies were going to let you go. It's not often they get the undivided attention of a handsome man."

Ellis turned Olivia in his arms. "So you think I'm handsome?"

Olivia opened her mouth, but no words came out.

Mrs. Davis came up behind the pair. "Now, now, none of that. Save it for when you have privacy. I never was one for public displays."

Ellis grinned at Olivia but let her go. "I don't suppose I could offer you ladies a ride home?"

Mrs. Davis beat them to the door.

"I take it that's a yes." Ellis ushered Olivia outside, then guided the two women to his car.

In short order, Olivia found herself in the back seat, the very small, confined back seat of Ellis's car while Mrs. Davis gave him directions to her apartment. Olivia smiled as Mrs.

Davis gave him directions that took them out of the way, extending the car ride. Olivia was also amused as Ellis hit the gas a few times and took the corners a little fast. By the time they were at Mrs. Davis's apartment, the older lady was grinning like a schoolgirl.

The pair walked Mrs. Davis to her apartment and saw her inside. Olivia had to brush a few tears back when Mrs. Davis told her that this was the best birthday party she had ever had.

Olivia took Ellis's arm in hers while they headed back to his car. "That was sweet of you."

"For a while there, I thought she was going to take us out to the highway for a joyride." Ellis helped Olivia into the passenger seat.

"I did, too. But either way, it was sweet."

Ellis leaned into the car, placing a kiss on Olivia's upturned mouth. "So are you."

Just that light kiss had Olivia's blood humming. A year ago she wanted to believe Ellis was just another shallow playboy. And though she still felt the playboy part fit him, he certainly wasn't shallow. And she knew he had never cheated on Lindsay during their on-again, off-again romance, so he knew how to be faithful. The problem was she still wasn't sure if he was the right man for her. Her body was sure he was, but her head was another matter. And with her heart involved, the situation could become complicated.

The drive from Mrs. Davis's apartment to Olivia's was a

short one. Ellis didn't bother to ask but got out of the car and opened the door for Olivia. He wanted a few more minutes alone with her. He'd been wrestling all week about what to do about her. He was attracted, of that he had no doubt. He'd been attracted to her a year ago. But she could be prickly, difficult, and argumentative. But as he had seen tonight, and had seen hints of it before, she could be sweet, sensitive, and loving.

"You don't have to walk me over." Despite her words, she tucked her arm into his and led him to her apartment.

"It's late." Ellis took her keys and opened her door.

"Yes, it is. And you shouldn't leave your car unattended too long in this neighborhood." Olivia gave him a half-smile and closed the door behind him when he preceded her inside. She watched as he gave the small apartment a once-over.

"I won't argue with you on that one. But I did want to talk to you." Ellis went and stood by the window that looked out into the parking lot. He could see his car from here. He wasn't taking any chances.

Olivia took off her coat and hung it up on a hook by the door. "About what?"

Ellis looked over at her. "About seeing you again."

Olivia's heart started to race. "You think that's a good idea? You could hardly wait to get rid of me before."

"I've since changed my mind. Come here." Ellis leaned up against the windowsill, half sitting on the small ledge.

Her heart still racing, Olivia obeyed. When she got

within arm's distance, he took her hand and pulled her to him. She closed her eyes when his head bent down to hers.

Thighs spread, Ellis pulled Olivia against his body. He cupped her chin and kissed her. He hadn't forgotten her taste or the feel of her against him. When his tongue probed and asked for entrance, Olivia moaned in the back of her throat and opened for him.

Time stood still, a cliché she knew, but it felt like it. She braced her hands on his chest and let herself drown in the passionate kiss. All she knew was Ellis's taste, Ellis's touch. His breath was coming in sharp exhalations, as was hers. She could feel his heart pounding under her palms. And when his hands trailed down her back, cupping her bottom, she allowed him to pull her further into his embrace.

Ellis lifted Olivia against him, wishing this interlude could reach its ultimate destination. But oddly, he wasn't quite ready yet, and he knew she wasn't. With regret, he released his hold on her, taking a moment for one last touch, one last taste.

"Dinner. Next Saturday. Seven." Ellis barely got out the words.

Still a little dazed, Olivia nodded. Then she realized what she was agreeing to. Taking a step back, she wrapped her arms around her waist and clenched her thighs together to ease the ache. Neither of them said anything else as she watched Ellis lock and close the apartment door behind him.

Olivia slid to the floor where she stood, her legs rubbery. She scarcely believed she had accepted a dinner invitation from him. But given the ferocity of their kiss and the way she'd melted against him, it would be silly to play coy now. Ready or not, she seemed to have started a relationship with Ellis Wallace.

Chapter Five

"You still with us?" Jack Warner propped his hip against the cubicle wall where Olivia was staring off into space.

Olivia jumped. She realized she had completely zoned out. Given the fact that Jack was six feet five and it was impossible to miss him, she was definitely not in her right mind. "No, I guess not. Sorry."

"I have an assignment for you. I promised them my best hacker. But I'm not so sure you're it right now." Jack took a seat in the chair opposite Olivia. "I'd ask what your problem is, but I'm pretty sure it's a six-foot-one male with dark hair and eyes."

Despite Jack being part-owner of the firm she worked for, and her immediate boss, she and Jack had become friends. He didn't have his boss face on now, but his friend one. She tossed down the pen she'd been fiddling with. "Yeah, he's a problem. I guess I'm trying to figure out why."

"I can tell you, having lived through what you're going through now, and being on the other side, just go for it." Jack had been plenty distracted himself when his now wife, Theo, had started working here, and he wanted to ask her out in the worst way.

"That's a very male attitude. I don't just go for stuff." Olivia swiped at the hair that was hanging in her face. She usually tied up her hair when she worked.

"And you have a very female attitude. You want to overthink it. You feel what you feel. And if you're lucky,

Ellis feels what you feel."

Olivia leaned back in her chair, exasperated with herself. "I guess I don't know exactly what I feel, any more than I know what he feels. It's different for men. And he's not exactly the shy, retiring type. He's dated half the women in the city."

"Only half the rich ones. Ellis has good taste. But don't sweat it. Selena is worried about him, so that means Theo is worried about him, too. And because they're worried, Isabelle is worried." Jack shook his head a bit, thinking about his wife and the wives of his friends.

Olivia grinned. "I think maybe I should go to them for advice on my love life."

Jack just nodded. "No doubt. So about the assignment. It's in your inbox."

Olivia opened it up. She had a dozen unread emails. She'd been staring off into space for a while. She and Ellis had gone out a few times in the last month, but there had been no repeat of the steamy kiss they'd shared in her apartment. It was as if Ellis had hit the brakes on their romantic relationship and they were back to being friends. Only his obviously restrained kisses at the end of their dates kept her hope alive. He was working hard at keeping his hands to himself. The question was why.

"It's routine, but Selena wants the best on this one." Jack turned Olivia's monitor so he could see it.

"And she's okay with it being me?" Since she started dating Ellis, she had been uncomfortable around Selena.

Though they weren't friends, Olivia respected Selena and what she'd accomplished. And though it was still a secret between her and Jack, Selena helped put black market antiquities dealers behind bars.

"Since Ellis was shot, she's been overly cautious. She did the background check on the guy who shot him. She's still feeling guilty."

Olivia, on behalf of Jack, had run a background check on the man who had shot Ellis. It had been her pleasure to do so. "He was a pro. His background was airtight. She has nothing to feel guilty about."

"I've told her that, but she's sensitive about it. Please run it and send it on over. He's potentially a huge client for her."

"And she's a huge client for us. Got it."

Jack nodded and rose. "As far as Ellis goes, just wait him out. He's not been his old self since he was shot. He'll come around. And maybe then you'll be able to focus again."

Unable to resist, Olivia responded. "How do you know so much about our relationship? I haven't talked about it."

"Selena says Ellis comes home alone after your dates. I'd say the frustration level between the two of you is in the red zone."

Slightly embarrassed, Olivia turned her monitor so she could hide behind it. Figures Selena would be keeping an eye out. And not surprising she'd tell Jack. Now that the two of them were happily married, and not to each other, their friendship had taken on a different tone. Olivia was sure there had been a thing between Selena and Jack, but it hadn't gotten far. The whole office had speculated on their romance, but Jack married Theo, and Selena married Carter, and the old gossip had died.

But Olivia was envious. Jack had met and married Theo in a very short time. They hadn't been married a year when their daughter was born. Jack had been thrilled. Olivia liked seeing the pair together. Theo was an attorney and rented office space in the building, so the pair were often seen together during lunch, and sometimes Jack didn't come back on time. It wasn't difficult to surmise what the pair were doing when they snuck off.

At the end of the day, that's what Olivia wanted. She wanted to be able to sneak away with the man she loved in the middle of the day. She'd like to come home to that same man night after night. And the older she got, the more her biological clock was telling her it was time to have babies. Olivia hadn't wanted children with her husband, but she'd had more than one fantasy about having them with Ellis. And thinking about sneaking off with him on her lunch break kept her mind straying from her work.

Grateful for the distraction, Olivia dove into the assignment for Selena. The background check was routine, one Olivia had run for numerous clients while working for Jack. In this digital age, people were not always who they claimed to be.

It took the rest of the day to get the file together for Selena. The potential client wasn't as squeaky clean as he'd like Selena to believe, but he wasn't the worst Olivia had seen. He wasn't interested in providence as he was interested in collecting, but Selena would keep him on the straight and narrow, or he wouldn't be a client. Olivia gave her approval and sent it. It wasn't but a few minutes before her computer pinged. Selena wanted to chat.

"Business or personal?" Olivia responded to the video invite, smiling at Selena.

"Figured it out, did you?" Selena brushed back her bangs, watching Olivia's face.

"You sent that file to Jack so that Jack would come talk to me about a bogus assignment and give you an excuse to contact me about Ellis." Olivia leaned back in her chair.

"Okay, so we're obvious. I've been worried about Ellis, and he seems to be more interested in talking to you than me, at least about personal stuff."

"At least you gave me a challenging bogus assignment. Ellis is fine. He looks like he could use a few more pounds, and if I had to guess, I'd say he could use more sleep. But I'm not sleeping with him, nor is he confiding his secrets to me. If you want your questions answered, ask Ellis."

Selena let out a frustrated breath. "He's uncommunicative these days. Tells me to mind my own business, in the way he does when I'm pushing too hard. But I do owe you some thanks. He's better than he was, and if nothing else, thinking about you keeps his mind off the shooting."

"You can tell any interested parties that he's well on his way to a full recovery. And if I become worried about him,

I'll let you know. How about that?"

Selena gave her a slight smile. "I guess it's better than Jack and me giving you a new assignment every week. Thanks, Olivia."

"You're welcome. And if you need me for any other security jobs, let me know." Olivia closed the chat. She wondered if Ellis appreciated how much his friends cared about him.

Olivia closed up her laptop and tucked it in her bag. If she didn't hurry, she'd miss the last bus out. After changing her shoes to her more comfortable sneakers, she went outside and headed toward the street. When a loud beep from nearby caused her to turn, she saw Ellis leaning against his car, waiting for her.

"Want a ride?" Ellis smiled at her from across the parking lot.

Smiling back, Olivia nodded. "What are you doing here? We're not supposed to go out until Sunday. You promised me a trip to the beach."

"I did. But that was just a ruse to see you in a bikini." Ellis handed her into the car.

"You're in for a disappointment. I'm more apt to wear my wetsuit."

"I should have known you surfed. The first time I met you, you showed up at the office looking like you had just come from the beach."

Olivia fastened her seatbelt. "I've been known to hit the beach before an assignment if it's later in the day. Jack keeps me busy; I rarely make time anymore. Do you surf?"

"No. I think it's something you're born into. I was born in the Midwest. No oceans. You're a California girl, through and through."

She wasn't sure if that was a compliment or not, but he'd been smiling when he said it. When she stopped and thought about it, other than their comparable computer skills, they had very little in common. So far, they didn't watch the same movies, didn't listen to the same music, and she hated sports while he loved them. She loved Italian food, while he preferred more exotic fare, though they both loved seafood.

"Would you like to have dinner?" Ellis interrupted her thoughts.

Settling more comfortably into the seat, she nodded. They were almost at his house when she realized where they were going. "I thought we were going out?"

"I said dinner. You fed me enough; I thought it was time to return the favor. Do you mind?" Heated eyes turned her way.

Olivia swallowed. "No, it's fine."

"Good." He pulled up to the gate and punched in the code.

Olivia couldn't help but look at the main house when she exited the car. She remembered Selena saying he'd been coming home alone.

"Something wrong?" Ellis took her arm and led her to his front step. He disabled the alarm and ushered her in.

"Not exactly. Let me tell you over dinner." Olivia set her

bag down and followed Ellis to the kitchen. She hadn't been in his house since they stopped working out together; she wasn't sure why she thought it would change during her absence, but it was still very much the same.

It only took half an hour to get dinner together. Olivia chopped veggies for the stir-fry Ellis was making. Ellis tossed everything in a pan, then dumped in some oil and seasoning, and poured the contents of the pan over rice. It was a bit spicier than she was used to, but it was delicious.

"I see you've kept up on the diet." Olivia took one last bite before setting her fork aside.

"With a few modifications. I have to admit, I'm not much on leafy vegetables. I've opted out of the kale and spinach. So what was it you were going to tell me over dinner?" Ellis took a sip of the wine he'd poured for them. He had noticed quickly that Olivia wasn't one to order alcohol but would drink it if it was in front of her. He was hoping to mellow her out a little. She'd been tense since she stepped into his home.

"I was thinking when we pulled up that Selena would know I was here. She and Jack are conspiring to keep tabs on you. They think I'm a good source of information. She gave me a bogus assignment today to check out a new client so she could ask about you. She mentioned she sees you coming home alone every night."

Ellis nodded. "There hasn't been a woman here since before I was shot. She thinks it's abnormal for me not to have had female companionship of the physical kind for the past three months."

Olivia took a large swallow of her wine. "If rumors are true, you're not one to go without. Physically, I mean."

Ellis took her hand. "I can't say I've been a saint in recent years. But I've had dry spells longer than three months. Believe it or not, I like to have some common ground, along with equal attraction, before I bring a woman home with me. It's best to set the ground rules of the relationship first before taking the next step."

Olivia looked at the strong hand that held hers. "Funny you should say that. I was thinking we don't have much in common. And it's been a long time since I played relationship games that needed ground rules."

"Given what happened with your husband, I can't say I blame you. You already know about my relationship with Lindsay. It took a long time to get involved with a different woman after we broke up the first time. I didn't feel single. She seemed to have the same problem, which is probably why we kept getting back together."

"So is that what this dinner is about? Setting ground rules?" Olivia pulled her hand from his.

"Sort of the opposite. You make me want to forget the rules." Ellis rose and rounded the table. He pulled Olivia to her feet.

Olivia didn't hesitate when Ellis pulled her into his arms and kissed her. She immediately went to her tiptoes to get a deeper taste. She felt Ellis's hands on her bottom, lifting her against him. She clamped her arms around his neck, her fingers fisting in his hair.

Ellis didn't need further invitation. His hands slid to her thighs and lifted her so that her legs were wrapped around his waist. It took him a few minutes to get them to his bedroom. He stopped multiple times along the way to press her against the wall and kiss her deeply. Her tongue played with his, and her thighs tightened around him. More than once he was tempted to take her where they stood. But somehow sanity reasserted itself. He didn't want their first time to be rushed in his hallway.

Olivia barely registered the feel of his bed against her back. She hadn't felt so much as an inch of separation between their bodies as he lowered her. She tightened her thighs around him, trying to pull him closer. Her body was on fire, and he'd yet to do more than kiss her, though his kisses were seductive and lured her deeper.

Ellis leaned back enough to pull Olivia's blouse off over her head, not bothering to unbutton it. She wore a lacy white bra underneath it. He watched as Olivia reached under her back and removed it herself.

"You're next." Olivia's hand went to Ellis's waist and grasped the hem of his t-shirt. Even in a plain black t-shirt, he was incredibly sexy.

"At least I don't have to explain the scars to you." Ellis rose to dispose of his jeans and briefs.

Olivia sat up and pulled her slacks off, leaving her matching white lace underwear in place. She didn't have the courage to pull them off as she stared at his exposed body.

Then she registered his comment. "Does it bother you? Me seeing them, I mean?"

"No. You've seen them before, and they didn't seem to bother you, except for the fact that you know how much it must have hurt. Right after I was shot, the woman I had been seeing came to see me. She was horrified, of course, about what had happened. But she seemed more horrified by the prospect of having to see the scars. She broke off our relationship."

Olivia sat up and touched the worst of his scars with her fingertips. "These don't somehow make you less of a man, less of a person. This was something done to you, not something you did."

Ellis placed his hand over hers. "I think that might be part of it. Feeling like a victim. It's not comfortable or something I had expected to feel. Had she not left, I'd have tossed her out had I had the energy."

Keeping her hand under his, Olivia got to her knees and walked on them to the edge of the bed where Ellis sat. She brushed several kisses across his chest, her hand over his heart.

Ellis lifted her so that she once again straddled his waist. He scooted back, pulling her with him. "There's certainly nothing wrong with your body. But I knew that before seeing you like this."

Olivia had no words as his hands found her breasts. He made her feel beautiful; made her feel like she had been made for him. His hands knew where to touch and how much pressure. His touch started soft and became firmer as he continued to make love to her. She once again felt the bed beneath her back, this time on her bare skin, as he rolled her over. His mouth traveled over her body, his hands taking their time as he stripped away the last scrap of her clothing.

Ellis paused only long enough to dig out protection and put it on. Everything about her body turned him on. Her skin was tan all over, her blonde hair dark against the white sheets of his bed. He found his fingers making patterns on her skin across her flat belly, the muscles defined by the hours she'd spent working out. He'd seen this body clad in her work out clothes, so its shape was no mystery. But the soft feel of her and the scent of her sweat-slicked body took his arousal to new heights.

Olivia found her hands trying to grip the muscles of his back, but the slight sheen of sweat made it difficult. She tried begging instead. "Ellis, please, no more."

Ellis's arms went under her back, as his fingers found their way to the nape of her neck. He slowly merged their bodies. Despite being shot, he still had to outweigh her by fifty pounds or more. He didn't want to hurt her.

Olivia adjusted her body under his, unable to lie still as his body invaded hers. Blindly her mouth found his, her teeth scraping his bottom lip. His lips left hers, and she felt his teeth scraping the soft skin of her neck as he lifted her and slowly thrust in and out of her. She lifted herself in time with him, straining to get as close as possible.

Ellis felt the clenching of her body and quickened his pace. He could feel her breath against his skin, but he couldn't hear it over the roaring in his ears. He could feel the sweat between their straining bodies, but he barely registered it over the intense pleasure he felt from being inside this woman.

Olivia wasn't sure if she could bear much more. She lifted herself again, and her body imploded. She held onto Ellis with all her strength as she rode out the intense waves of sensation that rocked her body.

Ellis thrust one last time into her before following her lead. In that moment, he was only aware of his body and the woman beneath him.

It was several moments before reality reasserted itself. Olivia couldn't find even a small hint of regret. When he didn't move, Olivia used her palms to wedge a little bit of space between her and Ellis. "Are you okay?"

Ellis chuckled. "Define okay."

Olivia found herself smiling at his satisfied tone. "I just wanted to make sure you didn't hurt yourself or anything."

"I might be a bit sore tomorrow, but right now I feel amazing. You're amazing." Ellis lifted his head so he could kiss her.

Olivia relaxed under his kiss, assured he hadn't hurt himself. When he hadn't answered her right away, she had been worried. "In case you were worried about it, you haven't lost your touch with the ladies."

Ellis rolled to his side. He pulled her slick body against

his. "I can't say I hadn't wondered. But I wasn't using you to find out."

Realizing he'd taken her seriously, she raised up on her arms, careful not to put too much pressure on his chest. "I think it's safe to say that this has been inevitable for a while now. I don't feel used. At least, not in a bad way."

Ellis pulled her mouth down to his again. He broke off the kiss when his interest started to become more than passing. "Good. I wanted to be sure. You're not like the other women I've dated."

Olivia took that as a good thing and settled down. "I hate to say this, but you should probably take me home soon. I have to work in the morning, and I can't go to work in the same clothes I wore today."

Ellis sat up. "I suppose I should have planned this better."

Olivia sat up but took the sheet with her. "How about you seduce me again on Friday night?"

Ellis pulled Olivia to her feet, taking in the sight of her nude body. "I think I can manage that. Go ahead and get dressed. If we lie here, I'm likely to fall asleep."

Olivia thought about asking him to stay the night with her but refrained. She didn't want to start being clingy and needy. Her body was still humming from his lovemaking, and she could use a little privacy to come to terms with what had just happened. Knowing something was inevitable and accepting the reality of it were not the same thing.

An hour later, Ellis left Olivia at her door. He kept the kiss chaste, knowing that if he took it any further, he would find his way into her bed. Instead, he bid her goodnight and drove home.

Olivia took a shower and slipped into bed, foregoing her nightgown. She fell into an exhausted slumber as soon as her head hit the pillow.

Chapter Six

Ellis was in the middle of going through the reports that had come in on some new antiquities they were trying to acquire when his cell phone rang. His team had done a thorough job, which was nothing less than he expected. He took his gaze from the report and checked the incoming call. Frowning, he ignored the call. Lindsay was the last person he wanted to talk to right now. Anytime she called him, it was because she wanted something from him. But she was married now, and anything she might need she should be going to her husband for.

He glanced up at the clock. It was almost five. He was supposed to pick Olivia up from work. He planned to feed her, then take her back to his place. He was planning on spending the entire weekend naked in bed with her. She seemed more than willing if her response to his lusty text earlier in the day was any indicator. It was Friday, and he had the next forty-eight hours to indulge his baser needs. Just remembering Olivia in his bed was enough to set his body on fire. He hoped dinner would be a quick affair.

He was halfway to his car when his phone rang. Seeing Lindsay's number again had him hitting the ignore button again. The last thing he wanted to do on his way to pick up Olivia was talk to his ex. Ever since she had announced her engagement, he had felt free from her in a way he hadn't felt before. She had been the one to break it off with him time and again, but it was he who now just wanted to move on, and he'd felt that way for the past year and a half.

When he pulled up in front of the office building where Olivia worked, she was already waiting for him. He saw her wave to someone inside before making her way to his car. He watched with deep appreciation as the skirt she wore rode up her thigh as she slid into the passenger seat.

"Sorry, I'm late." Ellis leaned over and kissed Olivia.

Releasing the seat belt she had been ready to fasten, she twisted her body so she could get a little closer. She pulled his head closer and heard him curse when he leaned over the gear shift to brace himself. She released her grip on him. "Sorry about that."

Ellis saw the mischievous look on her face and leaned over again to kiss her roughly. "You might want to be careful if you want to use that later."

Olivia sat back in her seat. "I'll be sure to remember that next time. I definitely have plans for that."

Ellis shuddered but put the car into gear and headed toward the restaurant where he'd made reservations. "How was work? Any more bogus assignments?"

"Not today. And I think my being at your house tonight will put any speculation about your health to rest."

Ellis glanced at her and grinned. "Selena has cameras in her house, same as I do, so she sees me coming and going. No doubt she'll be monitoring them after your visit the other night."

It was somewhat odd to think they were being watched,

but it wasn't as if Selena could see what went on behind closed doors. "I do have a new assignment coming up next weekend. Security detail for a fundraiser for The Heart's Way Foundation. You used to attend with Selena. Will you go?"

Ellis was not happy to hear she had another security job. The Heart's Way Foundation was a charity that helped fledgling foundations with their charitable projects and spearheaded many of its own. Selena was a big donor, and sometimes spokesperson, for the foundation, so Ellis had attended many events over the past few years. Ellis was also friends with John and Isabelle, who headed up the fundraising for the foundation, and they were not shy about pulling in friends. Previous events he had attended as Selena's bodyguard. Her husband Carter now did the honors. Ellis realized he had forgotten all about it. He had an invitation to attend as a guest this time. If Olivia weren't working, he would have brought her.

But even if he hadn't planned on attending, he would be now. Though there wasn't any real danger in attending the fundraiser, a lot of money was involved, and a lot of celebrities attended, so it was best to be prepared just in case. Jack did the security for free as his contribution to the foundation. He and his wife, Theo, would most likely be attending if they could find a sitter.

"Are you?" Olivia saw Ellis's jaw clench and realized he wasn't happy. She turned away from him. He would just have to deal with it.

"Yeah. I had forgotten. I'll have to get my tux to the cleaners this week." He didn't press the topic, not wanting to completely tick her off before their meal.

Silence descended. Olivia twisted the strap of her purse in her hands. Unable to sit, she turned back to Ellis. "I told you I was training for security."

"And I told you I didn't like it and wouldn't help. I haven't changed my mind."

"That's because you're incapable of changing your mind, of being reasonable."

"Oh, I can change my mind all right. But not about this. You're not cut out for it. You're too short, and despite working out, you're not strong enough to take on a man twice your size."

"Neither are you." Olivia wasn't backing down on this.

Ellis eased the car into the parking lot of the restaurant. "Face it, there are not that many people twice my size. You can't say the same."

"So now what? You think you can boss me around because we had sex?"

Ellis gritted his teeth against what he wanted to say to her. He had forgotten the feisty Olivia who hadn't made an appearance since he'd relented and let her work out with him. "No, I don't think that. I told you how I felt long before the sex."

Olivia relented. "I know. I'm sorry. Do you want to take me home?"

Ellis figured he had a couple of options. He went with the

first.   He opened the car door and went around to the passenger side. He opened the door and held out a hand. "No, I don't want to take you home. At least not to yours."

Olivia looked up at him. Though his jaw was clenched, he looked like he meant it. She put her hand in his.

Ellis closed the door, but instead of leading her inside, he pressed her against the car. He used his hips to pin hers. Not caring if anyone saw him, he slid his palm from her waist to the outside of her thighs beneath her skirt. "You'd do better to use sex to talk me into accepting your bodyguard assignment. I have a feeling it would work."

Olivia was a bit startled by the bold, intimate touch of his hands on her, but was not unduly surprised by the erection she felt pressed against her. Feeling bold, she slid her hand between their bodies, the back of her hand rubbing against him. "You think?"

Ellis shuddered and pulled back. "Yes, I think. Let's eat."

"We could order a pizza from your place." Olivia put her hand in his as he led them slowly to the restaurant.

"Too much of a hassle. Ordering pizza from behind a gated estate isn't as easy as you'd think. Unnerves the drivers."

Olivia imagined him driving naked to the gate after torrid lovemaking to pick up the pizza. She supposed he had a point. "Don't order anything that takes a long time."

Ellis gave her a hooded look. "Same for you."

Olivia stifled a giggle when Ellis kept her in front of him as the hostess led them to their table. She had no doubt he was still trying to get himself under control. But mostly she was happy they survived their first quarrel without too much damage done. She wasn't happy he felt the way he did, and he wasn't happy she wasn't going to back down. She imagined they'd have this fight again. She could only hope it ended the same way.

Olivia enjoyed their meal. They talked about the foundation a bit and the upcoming party. They talked about the new workout routine Olivia was working on. They talked about food, wine, travel, and just about anything else to keep their minds off what would happen later that night.

"Excuse me for a minute." Ellis rose.

"Sure. I'll see if the waiter has our check." Olivia watched as Ellis headed toward the men's room. She flagged down the waiter and asked for the check.

After the waiter left to get the check, she heard Ellis's cell phone ring in the pocket of his jacket. Figuring it couldn't hurt, she snagged the jacket and pulled out the phone. Her heart sank to her stomach when she saw who was calling.

When Ellis came back, Olivia was watching him, holding his cell phone in her hand. "Someone called?"

Olivia set the phone down beside her plate. She was desperately trying not to let out the anger and jealousy she was feeling in her tone. "Why is Lindsay calling you?"

"I don't know. That would be the third time today she's called. But I'm guessing you know that." He took the phone and slipped it back into his suit jacket.

Olivia was quiet for a moment. "Does she do that often?"

Ellis took cash from his pocket and set it beside the check. It would cover their meal and a big tip. "Let's talk about this outside."

"I'm not going to make a scene." Despite her words, Olivia let Ellis take her outside.

"To be clear, no, she doesn't call me often. Since her engagement, we have barely spoken. She came to invite me to her wedding. I went to the wedding. That's the last time I saw or spoke to her."

Olivia halted him with a hand on his arm when he brushed past her. "I'm sorry. I don't mean to be suspicious. It's just that this thing between you and Lindsay has gone on for years."

"I don't date married women. And I only date one woman at a time. It seems to me that you and I have been exclusive for over a month now. I'm not seeing Lindsay on the side."

Olivia was immediately contrite. "I didn't mean to imply you were. I know you're not the kind of man to cheat. But Lindsay is a bit of a sore spot for me when it comes to you. Surely you can understand that."

He could understand it, but he hadn't liked seeing suspicion in her eyes. "All right. Let's go."

Olivia kept quiet on the drive back to his place. She supposed she was to blame for most of their evening's disastrous moments. She knew how he felt about her wanting to be a bodyguard, so she should have waited to tell him. And she knew he wasn't seeing Lindsay anymore, though she didn't like the fact that the woman felt she could call Ellis whenever she felt like it. She was married now and had no claim on him. But the fact that Ellis had wanted her in the past, and part of him probably still did, was a hard pill to swallow.

"Want a drink?" When they got inside, Ellis went to the cabinet where he kept a bottle of Scotch.

"No thanks." Olivia followed him. She let him take a swallow before she put her hand on his to stop him from pouring a second.

Ellis swore but set the bottle down. "I don't know how we got so off track."

Olivia was willing to take the blame. "I've always had a bit of a temper, and you already know I don't always keep what I think to myself. I wanted tonight to be a repeat of our last night together."

Ellis cupped her chin, tipping her lips to his. He kept the kiss soft, savoring the taste of her. The other night, he had been frantic to have her, his desire for her so pent up. But tonight, he wanted it to be different.

Olivia melted against him as he kissed her. It seemed as if he could go on kissing her forever. His lips played with hers, coaxing her mouth open so his tongue could toy with hers. His fingers danced up and down her spine through the fabric of her blouse, bringing her body ever so slowly against his in the process.

Olivia surrendered to him. He took his time undressing her right there in the kitchen, slowly unbuttoning her blouse and kissing her skin as he exposed it. She felt her skirt drop to the floor when he unhooked it, his fingers drawing patterns on her belly and thighs. When his fingers slipped beneath the waistband of her underwear, he had to hold her up when her knees gave way.

Ellis swept her up in his arms, striding toward the bedroom. He stripped away the last of Olivia's clothing before removing his own. He set out to tease and arouse her. His mouth made the same path across her breasts, belly, and thighs that his hands had. He wanted to imprint himself on her, to show her there was no other woman, that she wasn't a substitute for Lindsay. Perhaps there was a time in the past when that might have been true, but at this moment, with this woman, Olivia was all he could think of. There were no others.

Olivia could scarcely move, other than to move restlessly on the bed while Ellis made love to her. He made a feast of her body, coming back time and again as if he would never be satiated. When she would have begged, he kissed her and stilled her words. He used his fingers to bring her to her first peak.

Ellis kissed her, stealing her cries. "Again."

Olivia didn't think it was possible, but Ellis showed her how wrong she was. He continued to tease and torment her until she was writhing under him. He stilled her hands with his hips, donned the condom he had left on the bedside table, and thrust into her heat. She was so hot and tight he thought he'd go mad. He lifted her hips and waited until she had reached her second peak before he let himself go and joined her.

Olivia felt tears sting her eyes, and feeling foolish, she quickly wiped them away. Everything about this man reached her to her very core. She was so madly in love with him that she felt like she would burst with it.

Ellis saw the tears, but instead of commenting on them, he kissed them away. He turned on his side, bringing her against his chest. He stroked her hair when she pressed her cheek to his chest.

Olivia sighed and fully relaxed in his arms. At that moment, nothing else mattered.

* * *

Olivia was rudely awakened by the shrill sound of a phone ringing. Ellis rolled over so he could grab his phone. It was after midnight, and he couldn't imagine anyone calling him so late, other than Selena. But it was not Selena on the other end; it was Lindsay again.

Reluctant to answer it but wondering what could be so urgent that she'd call after midnight, he answered. "Hello, Lindsay."

Olivia stiffened against him, but she didn't pull away. She glanced over at the clock on the nightstand. It was well after midnight.

"Calm down. Try that again, but slower this time." Ellis sat up and turned the bedside lamp on. He kept a pen and paper nearby, and he grabbed them. "When did he go missing?"

Olivia sat up, listening intently to the conversation. The word missing got her attention. She watched Ellis's face and realized he was serious.

Ellis scrubbed his hand over his face. "Did you call the police?"

Olivia could make out some of what Lindsay was saying on the other end of the line. It sounded as if Lindsay's new husband had gone missing. Lindsay had received some sort of email, but that was all she could make out.

"All right. I'll be over." Ellis climbed out of bed and looked around for his jeans.

Olivia climbed out of bed, but most of her clothes were in the other room. "What happened?"

"All Lindsay could get out was that Bennett was missing and that she'd received an email with a picture of him tied up." Ellis pulled on a fresh pair of briefs and yanked on his jeans.

Bennett Rogers was a very well-known movie producer. He'd been behind several hit movies in the past year. Olivia had heard several rumors about him that involved gambling, prostitutes, and drugs. Lindsay had told the family that the rumors were just that. She said there was no proof to any of them. Olivia hadn't bothered to check out the rumors. It was none of her business. Lindsay was friends with her sister Mandy, not her.

Olivia looked over at Ellis again while he finished

dressing. "You ran a full background check on Bennett, didn't you?"

Ellis glanced up as he fastened his boot. "No, why?"

Olivia's head jerked up in surprise. "He married your ex. I figured you must have checked him out."

"It might come as a surprise to you, but I don't care what Lindsay does. I had no reason to run a background check on her fiancé. She was free to marry whoever she wanted." He kept to himself the fact that he had run a cursory one when they first got engaged.

"I just thought, given your history and the rumors, you would have."

Ellis crossed the room. He loomed over Olivia. "You seem to be laboring under the impression that I still have feelings for Lindsay. I admit I care about her, but I'm not in love with her anymore."

Olivia wanted to point out that he was getting dressed after midnight to rush to his ex's side, but she refrained. He might not think he still had feelings for her, but his actions said otherwise.

Ellis stepped back when Olivia remained silent. "I'll be back as soon as I can."

"I'm going with you."

"It's late. There's no reason to."

Olivia made an unladylike sound. "I guarantee you Lindsay has already called Mandy, and Mandy and Baxter are now plastered to her side. You'll want a referee."

Ellis thought she might have the right of it. "All right.

You know everyone is going to know about us?"

"I'm not worried about it. Are you?" Olivia planted her hands on her hips.

Though not the response she was looking for, Ellis was more amused and aroused than angry. He stomped his boot on the rest of the way and came back to where Olivia was standing, battle-ready. He slipped his hands over hers, cradling her body to his. He backed her up until the back of her knees hit the bed. He blatantly rubbed his hips against hers, showing her his renewed interest.

Biting back a moan, Olivia slipped her hands from under his and wrapped them around his neck to keep her balance. "We shouldn't do this. We have to go."

He bit her lip, much as she had done to him earlier, and then released her. He was surprised by his quick physical reaction to her. And though he had made love to a woman more than once in a single night before, she lit his fuse much faster. He'd already made love to her twice since they'd made it back from dinner, and here he was ready to go again.

Olivia took a step back, her breath heaving. "Let me run a brush through my hair after I find my clothes and get dressed, and I'll be ready to go."

They were about twenty minutes into the drive when Olivia realized they were heading in the wrong direction. "My father's house is north of here."

Ellis gave her a puzzled look. "Why would we go to your father's house?"

"You really haven't been talking to Lindsay much, have

you?" Olivia still found it a bit hard to believe.

"No. Why?"

"She sold her house. Bennett also sold his. They're staying with my dad. My father just loves Bennett and offered to let them stay with him and my stepmother until they buy a new one. They've been house hunting since before their marriage. Apparently, they haven't been able to find what they want."

Ellis turned north and followed Olivia's instructions. "So I guess having Mandy and Baxter over isn't a big deal."

"My sister loves her parents' estate. She's holding out to inherit it one day. Mandy and Baxter are frequent visitors. And since Baxter and Lindsay are brother and sister, Mandy likes to entertain her husband and best friend at her parents' house."

"What about you?" Ellis realized Olivia hadn't talked much about her father, or Mandy for that matter. Olivia knew about his adversarial relationship with her half-sister, but overall, Olivia had been silent on the subject of her family.

"You'll see when we get there." It was all she was going to say on the subject. Her relationship with her family was complicated, and her affair with Ellis wasn't going to go over well.

Chapter Seven

It was a bit chaotic when they arrived. Baxter was in his wheelchair by the fireplace, with Mandy sitting on his lap, her auburn hair tousled from sleep. Lindsay was pacing the living room in an almost sheer nightgown with only a thin robe covering it, her dark hair flowing behind her as she paced. Olivia saw her father, Winston, seated in his favorite recliner, watching Lindsay pace. Olivia saw her father's wife, Regina, across the room, her eyes full of concern.

"Thank goodness you're here. I didn't know where else to turn." Lindsay threw herself into Ellis's arms.

Ellis patted her hair, a gesture he'd done hundreds of times during their relationship. "You should do what I'm going to do, and that's call the police. Gather up whatever evidence you have that someone took Bennett. The police will need access to his financials, his calendar, and whatever else you think might help figure out who took him."

"We can't go to the police." Winston rose from his recliner.

Ellis watched everyone turn his way. "And why is that?"

"Bennett got himself into some trouble. The police are likely to arrest Bennett if they find him."

Lindsay turned up her wet, pleading eyes to Ellis. "Please. You've got to help me. There haven't been any ransom demands or any other emails. There was just one showing him tied up somewhere. He hasn't been home in two days.

I'm scared."

Ellis led her to the sofa. "All right. But I make no promises. If I think it's best, I will contact the police."

"Always did have to have things your way." Mandy stood up from Baxter's lap. She came around and sat beside Lindsay.

Olivia stepped forward. She didn't think anyone even noticed her standing behind Ellis. "Now is not the time."

Mandy's angry eyes landed on Olivia. "What are you doing here? No one called you."

Olivia folded her arms across her chest. "I was with Ellis when Lindsay called. Twice if I recall correctly."

Lindsay turned confused eyes to Olivia, then to Ellis. Olivia could tell when Lindsay finally put two and two together. She didn't have to wait long for the explosion.

"Why, you little tramp!" Lindsay came at Olivia.

Ellis placed himself between the two women. "One more word out of you, and Olivia and I will leave."

Lindsay's mouth dropped open. "How could you? Of all the women, you picked Olivia?"

"You stopped getting a say in who I date when you broke up with me." Ellis took Olivia's arm from behind him and pulled her to his side.

Regina, usually the voice of reason, stepped into the fray. "Come now, Lindsay. You're just overwrought. Let Olivia help. She works for a private investigation firm. She's better suited to help you and has access to files that Ellis wouldn't. Between the two of them, I'm sure they'll find Bennett."

Ellis started to lose his patience when Lindsay burst into tears again, but was grateful when she didn't throw herself at him. She threw herself at Mandy instead.

Olivia stood back and watched the drama for a moment before speaking. "It will be ok. You should get Ellis what he asked for and get some rest."

Lindsay nodded and left the room, brushing against Olivia and knocking her back a step.

Olivia stayed Ellis's hand when he would have gone after her. "Let her be. She's upset."

"You shouldn't have come. You'll just make it worse." Mandy went back on the attack.

"And your attitude won't help." Olivia's gaze dropped to Mandy's stomach. Her brows furrowed. "You're pregnant."

"What was your first clue?" Mandy placed a hand over her belly, her face smug. "Baxter and I are very excited to be having our first child this winter."

Regina put an arm around Olivia. "We're all very excited, of course. And you'll be an aunt."

"Half aunt." Mandy went back to Baxter's side.

"Congratulations, both of you." Olivia tucked her hands into her skirt pockets. Her sister was more than halfway through her pregnancy, and she hadn't known.

"Thank you. Once we have Bennett back, the family will once again be complete." Baxter finally chimed in.

Ellis ignored the subtle reference. He and Baxter had never seen eye to eye. Never would. Baxter was one of the biggest reasons his relationship with Lindsay hadn't worked.

Lindsay adored her brother, and she found it difficult to go against him. Lindsay loved her brother more than she had loved him.

"I don't think there is much we can do tonight. Would the two of you like to stay?" Regina gestured to Olivia.

Olivia looked up at Ellis, who shook his head. "No, I don't think so. We can take what Lindsay has and start looking into Bennett's disappearance. I will need my laptop, and so will Ellis. And I can access the computers at work remotely from it."

It took a couple of hours for Ellis to go over possible scenarios with Lindsay. Olivia took notes and wrote down access codes to what Lindsay knew about. But given how recent their marriage was, Olivia would bet Lindsay didn't know everything about her husband's finances. For a man with the kind of money Hollywood producers made, these accounts didn't scratch the surface.

"We'll take what you've given us and get back to you as soon as we find something." Ellis stretched his back and yawned. He hadn't had a late night like this since before the shooting, and his body wasn't used to it.

"Are you sure you won't stay, Ellis?" Lindsay turned pleadingly to him.

"No. I'll get more done at home."

Olivia was more than ready to get out of the house. She wanted to say goodbye to Regina, but she had passed out on the couch. That left only the three of them awake. Mandy had claimed fatigue and said she needed her rest because of the baby. Baxter followed. Winston seemed disinterested in the whole affair and had headed to bed shortly after their arrival.

Olivia turned her attention to Lindsay, who was sulking on the couch, her gaze going back and forth between Ellis and Olivia. She rose and bid Lindsay farewell, knowing Ellis would follow suit.

"So what do you think?" Olivia took a deep breath of the night air.

"I'm not sure. Lindsay is convinced her husband has been kidnapped."

"Seeing your husband tied to a chair can certainly make one think that. But I'm not sold."

Ellis gave Olivia a surprised look. "You think it was faked?"

Olivia shrugged. "I don't know. He's a Hollywood producer. He'd have the resources. Something seems fishy, that's all."

"What worries me is that everyone is adamant that we don't go to the police."

"Lindsay has faith in you. No one else that she knows is better suited to find her husband."

Ellis wasn't so sure and said so. "She never liked my job and threw it in my face every time we argued. And when I went to work for Selena, she blew up."

Men could be so naïve. "Going to work for Selena had nothing to do with your ability. That was jealousy, plain and simple. Selena is beautiful, rich, and intelligent. She's exactly the kind of woman to attract a man like you, and you were practically living in her pocket."

"Selena was still legally married when I met her, and she had a thing for Jack. Nothing was going to happen between us. Not to mention, she was my employer."

"Doesn't matter. Lindsay doesn't like to share. Neither does Mandy, for that matter."

Ellis halted her. "What about you?"

"Let's just say if Lindsay keeps throwing herself at you, I might have to punch her."

Satisfied with that answer, he opened the passenger door but climbed in instead of holding the door for her. He handed her the keys. "I don't think I can see straight to drive. I still don't have all my stamina back."

"Really? I hadn't noticed." She gave him a lascivious grin and closed the passenger door.

Ellis relaxed against the seat as Olivia drove them back to his house. He recalled something that had bothered him earlier. "You didn't know your sister was pregnant?"

Olivia briefly glanced at him but kept her attention on the road. "No. But I guess it's not a big surprise. As you saw tonight, we're not exactly close. Our relationship is a bit complicated."

"What relationships aren't? Why the animosity?"

Olivia rolled her shoulders, answering him, though she'd rather have not. "My mom had an affair with her dad, and I was the result. Mandy was eight when I was born. And she wasn't happy when my mother forced our father to acknowledge me. Mandy was the only child of a very wealthy, very influential family. You can bet she didn't like sharing the attention. And when the scandal broke, she had to bear the brunt of a lot of unpleasant questions and gossip. And since my mother wasn't going to go away quietly, my father had no choice but to acknowledge me as his daughter. Lindsay adopted Mandy's attitude toward me. I was the younger, obnoxious sister who they wanted out of their hair."

"Regina didn't seem to mind your being there tonight."

"Regina is great. She was all for her husband claiming me as his daughter when she found out about me. She wasn't thrilled about the affair, of course. And she wasn't thrilled that he hadn't prevented the pregnancy. But she had two choices. She could dump her husband and move on, or she could accept what he'd done. Regina was pragmatic about the whole thing. He had an affair, he had another kid, so he'd better take responsibility. He was apologetic and did his duty. It seemed to satisfy Regina."

Ellis had noticed her father hadn't even said hello. "It doesn't seem like Winston was happy to see you tonight."

"Don't take it personally. He doesn't take an interest in much of anything. He let Regina raise Mandy, and when I was around, he made Regina take care of me. We rarely saw him. His presence tonight tells me he thinks this is the real deal."

"That's another thing that is bothering me. Why care about Lindsay so much? She's just his daughter's friend.

Mandy may be married to Lindsay's brother, but that doesn't quite explain it."

"Seriously? You didn't see the way my father ogled her tonight? He wants in her pants so badly; he practically salivates when she's in the room."

"She's young enough to be his daughter."

Olivia gave him an absent shrug. "Yes, but she's not. When Lindsay hit puberty, you can bet dear old Dad took notice."

"That's disgusting."

Olivia could only agree. "Agreed. But it would be worse if Lindsay were interested, but she's not. When she wasn't in love with you, she was in love with someone just like you. Even Bennett superficially looks like you. He's the same height, has the same color hair, and has the same skin tone. He's not as fit as you, and he doesn't have the same colored eyes, but if someone said the two of you were related, no one would argue. And he's rich, which is her number one requirement in a man."

Ellis thought about it but couldn't dispute that fact. "She wasn't always that way. I wasn't rich when we met. That came a little later. It was one of her more off-putting qualities."

"Money is a nice thing to have, but certainly not something to base a relationship on."

Ellis dropped the topic of money. "What about your mom? I can see Regina accepting a child, but not the woman who mothered it hanging around."

"Mom had her own life to live and had plenty of male companionship. She didn't force herself into the family mix. And she didn't miss him, that's for sure. The affair was short-lived. And she was much more careful going forward. There were no more children. But Mom's not a bad sort. She wanted to make sure I knew who my father was, and she loves me. She eventually settled down and married. I was in my twenties by then, but she's happy now. Her husband has two children. It's awkward between the three of us when we happen to get together as a family, but they all live on the other side of the country, so it's not often."

"Sounds like your mother and mine have a bit in common. My father didn't stick around to marry my mother when she got pregnant. She raised me. She got married when I was in my mid-teens. He's a great guy, though. She was young enough to have more children, so I have two younger half-brothers."

"I bet you were a handful." Olivia pulled into the private drive and punched in the code at the gate.

"Probably more so now than before. I didn't let Selena call her right away after I was shot. She's still pretty ticked off at me." Ellis opened the car door and was annoyed at how stiff his body was.

"Why not?" Olivia looked at him over the hood of his car.

"You'd have to know her. She would have fussed and driven the doctors crazy. Let's just say I wasn't up to fussing."

Olivia came to his side and let him lean on her a bit. He'd

hit the end of his rope. "You don't call this fussing?"

Ellis punched in the code to his front door. "Nope. You don't fuss. You demand. You push. And then you quietly do what has to be done. My mother would have driven me crazy within an hour of her arrival."

Olivia set the alarm behind them. She walked him straight to his bed. Ellis dropped onto the edge of the bed and stripped. Olivia helped him settle under the covers. He was asleep in moments. She touched the scar on his chest before pulling the blanket up.

Too restless to sleep, Olivia went into the living room and pulled out her laptop. She had questions about Bennett and what he had been involved in. Something about the kidnapping seemed wrong. Loan sharks and drug dealers didn't kidnap. They beat up or killed. And since there had been no ransom demand yet, money didn't seem to be the motivation. And for a man like Bennett, money was always the motivation.

* * *

Ellis woke up around ten. Groggy from the late night, he turned blurry eyes to the clock cand groaned. It had been a while since he'd had such a late night. It had been sometime after four when he'd finally climbed into bed. He rolled over to wake Olivia, but she wasn't there. Somewhat disappointed that his morning frolic was foiled, he climbed out of bed and headed to the bathroom.

A quick shower revived him, and he felt human again. He touched the scars on his chest, the sight of them still disconcerting sometimes. Instead of dwelling on them, he tugged a white t-shirt over his head and went in search of Olivia and coffee.

He found her in his living room. She was asleep on his couch, her laptop plugged in and running a program. Frowning, he came over and looked at the screen. She was running a background check on Bennett. The software looked sophisticated, but given who she worked for, that didn't surprise him. He went to his bedroom, grabbed an extra blanket, and came back to drape it over her. She was curled up in a ball, no doubt cold from lying uncovered for who knows how long. He let her be and headed for coffee.

When he finished making coffee, he went back into the living room. Olivia hadn't budged. He went and picked up her laptop, taking it with him to the kitchen. Idly sipping his coffee, he took a peek at what the computer had pulled up. There were phone records, associations he belonged to, bank account information, and his police record. Looked like their pal Bennett had some recent run-ins with the police, but nothing significant.

Curiosity had him poking around her laptop. He found the files she had on him. He already knew she had accessed his medical records, so that didn't surprise him. A month ago, he would have found it intrusive and been ticked off. Now he thought it was sweet. He also found the police report of the shooting, some footage from the internet, and the press release afterward. Despite the scars, sometimes it felt like it had happened to someone else.

"Find anything?" Olivia yawned, pushing her hair out of her face as she half-stumbled into the kitchen.

"No, I just started poking around. Bennett has a police record for soliciting a prostitute, a small drug charge, and an assault charge. Pretty typical stuff for a guy like him. Nothing he couldn't buy his way out of. I don't know what Lindsay sees in this guy."

"Charm. He oozes it." Olivia went to the coffee pot and poured herself a cup. She also brought the pot and gave Ellis a refill.

"Thanks." Ellis took a sip. "Nothing overt sticks out. But money will probably be the trail we follow."

"That's what I was thinking last night. Drug dealers and loan sharks aren't typically known for kidnapping. Too much risk. A broken arm or leg, or a bullet, is much simpler."

"Yeah. Kidnapping takes a lot of planning. I'll look over the photo to see if anything stands out, but I'm guessing not. I admit I wasn't completely awake last night while we talked to Lindsay, but I don't recall anything obvious."

"No. Me either. Not a hotel. Probably a house. Remote. But in the vast estates of Beverly Hills, it would be easy to smuggle in a body and no one is the wiser."

Ellis nodded. "And just as easy to smuggle a body out."

"That's true. You know, Lindsay might not thank you when she sees how deeply you start digging into Bennett's past."

Ellis wasn't worried. "I told her to go to the police. She's refusing. It won't be the first time she gets ticked off at me. But I think she knows something she's not sharing."

Olivia took a seat across from Ellis. "I got that feeling, too. Most people wouldn't call their ex-boyfriend to find their missing husband. But what bothers me is my father's statement that the police would be more likely to arrest Bennett than to help him."

"And no one disputed him, so everyone in that room knows something they're not sharing, and whatever it is, it didn't pull up in your search." Ellis picked up Olivia's hand and toyed with her fingers.

"If I can't figure it out, I'm sure you can. But you have a job, one that requires your attention. Being the vice president of a major corporation the size of Powell Trading doesn't leave you much free time."

"I got the feeling you were planning on helping me. But you have a full-time job, too. One that is getting busier by the day. If you keep taking on security assignments, you're not going to have much time to work on finding Bennett either."

"That was subtle." Olivia frowned at him but didn't pull her hand away. "All right. Tell you what. I won't take any more security assignments until we find Bennett. Happy?"

"Extremely." Ellis came around the table and scooped Olivia up in his arms. "Interested in a morning frolic before we get to work?"

Olivia wrapped her arms around Ellis's neck and giggled. "Definitely."

Their frolic was fast-paced and left Olivia limp and sweaty. Since Ellis had already showered, once Olivia could stand again, she used the shower while Ellis made breakfast. When she found her way back to the kitchen, she heard voices. One of them was Selena, and the other was a man she didn't know.

"You want to tell me why you're asking?" The unknown man's voice was low but carried.

"I can't yet. I will soon, I promise. I just need you to see if you can find anything illegal he might be involved in." Ellis glanced up and waved Olivia into the room.

"Hi." Olivia came around. She saw Selena smiling at her and knew what the other woman was thinking.

"Morning, Olivia. This is my husband, Carter."

Olivia held out her hand. The man was the opposite of his wife. About Ellis's height, but a little fuller in the chest. Dark hair, dark eyes. Not handsome but striking. He'd be a hard man to forget. "Nice to meet you. You're a detective with the LAPD, aren't you?"

"Yes. Which is why I'm a bit concerned that you and Ellis want me to run a criminal background check on Lindsay's husband but won't tell me why."

"I'll defer to Ellis on this one." Olivia ignored Carter's questioning look.

"How are you tied to this?" Selena took a sip of her coffee, completely pleased by the intimacy she saw between

Ellis and Olivia.

"Lindsay is best friends with my half-sister, Mandy. And Mandy is married to Lindsay's brother, Baxter."

"You're Mandy's sister?" Selena suddenly had doubts.

"Don't worry. They're not friends." Ellis saw Selena's eyes go cold. Selena didn't like Mandy at all, though she and Lindsay were friendly enough.

Selena relaxed. "Good. What exactly is going on?"

"I can't say right now." Ellis simply repeated the answer he'd given them earlier.

Carter relented. "All right. I'll check. But you have forty-eight hours to come forward with a plausible answer, or I won't be able to help. A background check on Bennett Rogers will trigger a few questions from my superiors. They give us a bit of autonomy, but I can't keep it a secret for long."

"Don't worry, I will. I appreciate your help. Olivia could dig up the info herself, but I'd like to keep her out of jail."

Carter took his wife's hand. "I heard rumors about you, Olivia. Word is you're a better hacker than our pal Ellis here. But I can't, in good conscience, let you dig into police files."

Olivia simply nodded. "Which is why I assume Ellis called you here. I ran a check through public records and found some minor stuff. But I'm guessing there's more to the story, and Bennett would have paid to cover it up."

"It's tricky to maintain complete secrecy in Hollywood. And we have a lot of celebrities, producers, and directors coming through our doors. But we do attempt discretion. I'll get back to you. My shift starts in a couple of hours. It will be a few more before I can get you what you want."

"Appreciate it." Ellis walked the couple to the door.

"So how will he explain running the check?" Olivia took a seat on the couch, tucking her legs under her.

"Probably say he got an anonymous tip that Bennett was involved in something. He'll play it low-key. But I will have to tell him soon. Lindsay is naïve if she thinks she can keep this a secret. There's no way of knowing what the kidnappers ultimately want. And there's no way of knowing how long they'll hold him, or if they plan on releasing him."

"People will notice he's missing." Part of Olivia's checks last night told her that Bennett was a social creature. He was usually out strumming up money or promoting some project he was working on. And he was always working on something.

"We'll wait on Carter and see what he finds and go from there. I'll start running the accounts Lindsay gave us last night. See if you can find any others she didn't."

Olivia grabbed her laptop and started digging. If Bennett had any hidden accounts or hidden assets, she'd find them.

Three hours later, Ellis answered his ringing phone. "Hi, Carter. Find anything?"

Olivia perked up in her seat and moved closer so she could hear what Carter was saying.

"Hold on a sec. I'm putting you on speaker." Ellis tapped the button on the phone and set it on the table so they could both hear.

Carter resumed his questions. "I said, where is he? Police in the county over are looking for him."

Olivia looked over at Ellis and simply waited.

Ellis answered. "We don't know. We're looking for him. What is he wanted for?"

The sound of tapping keys came over the line. "Hit and run. Seems he was coming home from a night of partying, and while still drunk, he decided to drive himself home. He hit a mother of two who was crossing the street after dropping her kids off. Thankfully she lived, but both her legs were broken, several of her ribs were broken, and she had a head injury. She had emergency surgery to release the pressure in her head from the bleeding. She's still in the hospital, but her prognosis looks good. According to the files, she'll be released in a few days."

Ellis cursed and rubbed the sore spot on his chest. "All right. Let me get back to my client. I'm strongly urging them to come forward and go to the police. If they don't, I will. I'll catch you back hopefully tomorrow. I appreciate it."

"It goes without saying that if you find out where he is, you'll give me a call. I don't want to have to arrest you for obstruction."

Ellis agreed. "And I don't want to make you arrest me. I'll be in touch. Thanks again."

Chapter Eight

"We need to tell my husband not to work you so hard."

Olivia heard the voice from across her desk and looked up for the first time in over an hour. She smiled at the woman in front of her. "Hi, Theo. How are you doing?"

Theo shifted her daughter from one hip to the other. "I was just popping in with the baby. I finished up with my clients for the day, and Patty and I are playing hooky. I just wanted to see how you were doing."

Olivia came around the desk and took Patty from Theo. She bounced the baby for a minute before tucking her to her chest. "Checking in on Ellis, are you?"

Theo set the diaper bag down on the floor and took a seat. "Am I that obvious? I heard a rumor you were dating him."

Olivia took a seat in her chair and bounced a giggling Patty on her knee. "I am, but you already know that from Jack and Selena."

"True. Guess I wanted to hear it from the source, and all that. We've all been worried about him. Glad to hear he's up and about. But really, you look tired. I should know. I haven't slept a whole night through since Patty was born."

"Between work and Ellis, I guess I haven't been getting much sleep." Olivia couldn't help but grin. She and Ellis had spent Saturday and Sunday finding out all they could about Bennett. When they weren't working, they spent the rest of the time rolling around Ellis's bed.

Theo smiled back, tucking a strand of honey-blonde hair behind her ear. "Well, well. Must be serious. I'm happy for you. Of course, Jack is now worried you'll take the job offer Selena made you last year."

Olivia glanced up at Theo, then back to Patty. "I didn't know he knew she offered me a job. I suppose Selena told him. But you can reassure Jack I don't plan to go anywhere. I'm not sure where this thing with Ellis will end up, but it won't end up with me working for him."

Theo rose and picked Patty up from Olivia's arms. "Can't say I blame you for that one bit. I love Jack, but I don't want to work with him, though I will admit it's nice working in the same building."

Olivia picked up Theo's bag from the floor and handed it to her. "Headed in to see Jack?"

"Yes. He was in a meeting, so I figured I'd come visit you first. I heard you're doing security for The Heart's Way fundraiser again. I imagine Ellis isn't happy he can't take you as his date."

"He's not happy at all that I'm doing security work. It's a bone of contention between us. But I didn't even think about going as his date when I took the assignment."

Theo bounced Patty, who was getting fussy. "By the way, there will be a big announcement from Isabelle and John. They're going public. But I wanted to tell you first."

That got Olivia's attention. She knew the couple well. They came into the office now and again to discuss business. Olivia had done some background checks for John a few times as well. The Heart's Way was a big client of Jack's. Olivia didn't socialize with the couple; she didn't move in their social circle, but she knew them well enough to be curious. "What kind of announcement?"

Theo smoothed back her daughter's hair. "This kind of announcement. I thought for sure Isabelle would wait a little longer before having a baby, but it seems she changed her mind."

Olivia wasn't surprised. She'd seen the heat the couple generated when they were within a few feet of each other. "They've been married, what, a year and a half?"

"Just a little over. I met Isabelle for the first time at her wedding. I was Jack's reluctant date."

Olivia knew the story of how Theo had met Jack. The entire office did. Theo was the daughter of Jack's business partner, Tom Landry, and he wanted Jack to protect his daughter from a former employer. They hadn't known each other long when they got married. And Theo got pregnant shortly after their wedding.

Olivia glanced at Patty. She then smiled at Theo. "I'm very happy for them. You'll have to invite me to the baby shower."

"You got it. Selena and I can't wait to get started. Isabelle and Selena threw mine, so I can't wait to return the favor."

Olivia sat back in her chair as she watched Theo head to Jack's office, her mind no longer on the task in front of her. When she had married Dennis all those years ago, she had imagined a happily ever after. What she had gotten was heartache and disillusionment. She wanted what Theo had. Theo and Jack were very different, but their marriage was rock solid. From what she had seen of Isabelle and John, they were devoted to each other and the foundation they worked for. Selena and Carter seemed very happy, though they had only been married a short while. Olivia couldn't help but envy the three women.

Now there was Ellis in her life. Here she was in a relationship with a man unlike any other she had met before. He made her start wondering if happily ever after was possible after all. They had only been lovers for a few days, but she was already in love with him. She wondered if she should try to put some distance between them, wondered if they had gotten too close too fast, but she figured her heart wouldn't be in it, so why bother. She wanted to see where this road would take her, even if it ended in heartache.

Olivia went back to work, but she couldn't quite get Ellis out of her head. Talking to Theo and playing with Patty made her think about what it would be like to marry Ellis and have children with him. How could it not? But time would tell what would become of her relationship with him. He had wanted to get married and settle down with Lindsay years ago. Perhaps he would be ready to try again with someone else. Namely one Olivia Knight.

Olivia gave a sigh, refocused on her job, typed in some new search parameters, and let the computer do its thing. Olivia had found the newly charged files on Bennett last night. It had taken the police a little time to go through the footage from the traffic cameras, but eventually, they had the vehicle information of who had hit the young mother of two. Olivia was surprised the arrest warrant had managed to stay under the news channels' radar but figured it was only a matter of time. Big time Hollywood producer involved in a hit-and-run would make for big news.

Olivia had also found some other accounts Lindsay hadn't mentioned. Olivia couldn't help but think she could live off the money in just one of those accounts and be set for years. He had more money in some of his other accounts than she would probably see in a lifetime.

Olivia heard a commotion on the other side of the office, but she didn't pay it much mind. She was wondering if Ellis was working on Lindsay's case or neck-deep in his work. He had told her he might be late but gave her a device so that she could get into the estate without him. She had been touched and a bit startled by the absolute trust that his giving her that device meant.

"You little bitch. You just couldn't pass up the opportunity, could you? Just like your mother, stealing another woman's man." The venomous words were spewed at Olivia from across the room.

Olivia's head popped up, recognizing Lindsay's voice. She got to her feet and was knocked to the floor when Lindsay's right hook caught her in the jaw. Stunned, Olivia sat on the floor.

"What did you think you were doing, coming with him Friday night? No one wanted you there." Lindsay's hand balled into a fist at her side. She paused in her tirade long enough to kick Olivia in the shin.

Olivia bit back a cry and got to her feet. "Are you crazy?"

"You're the crazy one." Lindsay slapped Olivia across the face, this time losing her balance as she swung. Lindsay went down on her knees, sobbing incoherently.

Olivia ignored the stinging of her cheek. She could feel a bit of blood gathering on her lower lip. "Come on. Get up."

Lindsay pulled away from Olivia's hand and got to her feet. She wobbled a bit but stayed upright. "You stole Ellis from me."

Olivia nodded at the security guard who was now standing a couple of feet from Lindsay. "I didn't steal Ellis from you. You broke up with him and married someone else. Did you think he would just sit around for the rest of his life, pining for you?"

"Yes! He's mine." Lindsay took a swing at the man who grabbed her, but she wasn't strong enough to get free.

"You've been drinking, Lindsay. It's no wonder with all the stress you're under. But attacking me isn't going to fix your problems." Olivia followed the guard as he escorted Lindsay from the building.

"What do you know about it? Huh? You probably orchestrated the whole thing. First, you took Ellis, and now you want Bennett. You think you're so smart. But you're just a tramp like your mother."

Olivia was tempted, very tempted, to punch the smirk from Lindsay's perfect face. "I suggest you shut up. You know nothing about my mother."

Lindsay fell against the nearby door. "I know she's the type to sleep with married men. I know you're just like her, taking Ellis from me. But I'll get him back, I swear it."

Olivia's head was pounding from the pressure of holding back her temper. "You can bet Ellis won't have you. Go home and sleep it off. Ellis and I will be in touch."

Lindsay screamed at Olivia, but Olivia just kept walking. Her face hurt where Lindsay punched her, and her shin wasn't in any better shape. She headed to the bathroom, knowing the security guard would put Lindsay in a cab and make sure she didn't get back inside. Once in the bathroom, she headed to the mirror. Her cheek was swelling under her eye, and her lip was split. She lifted her pant leg, but other than a bruise forming, there wasn't much damage.

Olivia washed the blood from her mouth and headed out. She went straight to the ice machine. That was where Jack and Theo found her.

"You should have that little witch arrested for assault." Theo kept her voice low so as not to upset Patty, who was sleeping on her shoulder.

Jack seconded the idea. "We have plenty of witnesses who saw her attack you. You can't let her get away with it."

Olivia just shook her head and wrapped some ice in a couple of layers of paper towels. It was the best she could do. "Lindsay is just upset."

"Because you're seeing Ellis?" Jack took Olivia's arm and led her toward his office.

Olivia sat on the sofa when Jack practically pushed her onto it. "There's a bit more to it than that."

Theo set Patty down in her car seat. "She hardly has any right to be upset."

Olivia took the glass of whiskey Jack poured for her and took a sip. She shuddered and coughed, not used to drinking anything quite so potent. "Bennett, her husband, is missing. She called Ellis on Friday night, and we went over there. It looks like someone kidnapped him, but there have been no ransom demands, and the kidnappers have not been in touch since they sent a single photo over. Lindsay wants Ellis to find him. I volunteered to help."

"You're a nicer person than I am. I'd have told her to go to the police and left." Theo sat next to Olivia and dabbed some antibiotic ointment on her cut lip.

"I've known Lindsay for so long; she's like family. Mandy and Baxter were there, as were my father and stepmother. None of them were very useful. Ellis came in and took charge. I figured if nothing else, I could act as a referee between Ellis and Mandy and Baxter."

"Why didn't they go to the police?" Jack took her empty glass and set it aside.

"Ellis enlisted Carter's help, and Carter found out Bennett has an arrest warrant for a hit and run. He ran his car into a young mother crossing the street a few days ago. They didn't want to go to the police because they didn't want him arrested. We found out about the warrant after Lindsay asked for Ellis's help. Ellis told Carter that if he found the man, he'd let Carter know so he could arrest him. So far, we haven't found him."

"I guess the real question is, was he kidnapped, or was it faked because he's wanted?" Jack went behind his desk and punched in his security code.

"I haven't quite decided on my theory to that question yet. Faking a kidnapping to get out of being arrested seems a bit farfetched. But we are talking about a Hollywood producer here. He would probably think it made for a great plot."

"Mmm. You might be right. What does Ellis think?" Jack pulled up a search program.

Olivia shrugged. "I think he leans toward it being faked. I've been digging into Bennett's financials, and Ellis is trying to find any digital trace of him so we can turn him over to the cops."

Jack glanced over at Olivia. "Anything in his financials raise any red flags?"

"No. He has a whole lot of money. It's almost sick how much. As far as I know, his recent movie projects have panned out, and no one in the tabloids has anything bad to say about him."

Jack went back to his screen. "Any drug charges, felonies, or anything like that?"

Olivia touched her sore cheek. "A couple of busts with prostitutes. You'd think Lindsay would be more upset about her husband cheating than Ellis moving on. There were also a couple of minor drug charges, but they were dropped. He also gets mean when he drinks, so there were some drunk and disorderly charges. You can add drinking and driving and reckless endangerment to that list."

"I trust that if anyone can find Bennett, you and Ellis can. But he just got back to work, and he's got to be swamped. It's not as if he's going to devote himself to the project."

Olivia realized where this was going. "Jack, I appreciate your help, but you have a wife and baby to pay attention to. I don't need your help tracking Bennett. And if I'm honest, I'm not working that hard on the project either."

Theo pressed a fresh bag of ice to Olivia's cheek. "No one would expect you to help. Lindsay is Ellis's ex-fiancée, and he doesn't owe her anything."

Olivia closed her eyes. "Try telling him that. He says he cares about her and is willing to help her find her husband. Lindsay is more than willing to use their past relationship to her advantage. You should have heard her shouting."

"As to that, I will." Jack pulled up the security footage. Lindsay was in the middle of the office, screaming that Olivia had stolen Ellis from her.

Olivia pressed her fingers to her temple. She groaned, now extremely embarrassed. "The whole office probably heard her ranting. And half of them probably saw her sock me in the jaw."

Jack tried to sound sympathetic, but he was too ticked off. "Only half. I want you to go home and get some rest. And I'm pulling you from the foundation's security detail on Saturday. I can't have you there with a busted face."

Olivia opened her mouth to protest, but her face hurt, and

she shut up. "I guess taking a hit from her doesn't look so good for my security skills."

Jack came from behind his desk and patted her shoulder. "I don't doubt that if you hadn't known her, you could have taken her."

Olivia tried to smile at his assurance, but her lip hurt too much. "Thanks. I think I will go home."

Olivia went back to her desk to fetch her purse and jacket. She tucked her laptop in her bag and did her best to ignore the curious stares from her coworkers as she exited the building. It was bad enough they had heard the awful things Lindsay had yelled at her. It was worse that they had watched her get punched.

When she got back to her apartment, she called Ellis.

"I'm almost done here. Are you off work early?" Ellis asked as he worked on a report.

"I'm at my apartment. I wasn't feeling well, and I left early." Olivia was glad Ellis couldn't see her. She knew her face was red from the bald-faced lie. He was right; she was a terrible liar.

"I could stop by and make you feel better." Ellis leaned back in his chair, his thoughts now totally focused on Olivia at the other end of the line.

"I can't say your offer isn't tempting, but I really don't feel good. And you shouldn't leave your car parked in my lot." That part was completely true.

"If you're sure. I can pick you up from work tomorrow. We should probably regroup on Bennett's case."

Olivia closed her eyes and leaned back against the couch. "There isn't anything else on my end. All his money is legit. He's rolling in dough, so unless he was kidnapped for a ransom, then money isn't the motivator. Hopefully, you have better luck tracing his movements than I have."

Ellis heard something odd in her tone. "I could pick you up tomorrow from work, and we could not discuss Bennett."

Olivia bit the good side of her lip. "That's okay. You can pick me up Friday, and I can spend the night with you then. You've got work to catch up on, and I need to catch up on my sleep."

"Friday?" Ellis's tone was flat.

Olivia nodded and realized he couldn't see her. By Friday, her lip and cheek should be all better. "Yes, Friday. The fundraiser is Saturday, so you'll be busy then."

"Fine. Friday." Ellis hung up the phone.

Olivia climbed to her feet and headed to the bathroom for some pain reliever. She knew Ellis was angry with her for refusing to see him for the rest of the week, but it was for the best. She could only hope Ellis would find Bennett before then.

* * *

Ellis tried to rein in his temper, but it was a losing battle. He wasn't sure why Olivia was refusing to see him. Last night he thought they had left on a positive note. He had not wanted to take her home, and she had been reluctant to leave, but they both had to work in the morning, and Olivia didn't have her things with her to get ready. The suit she had worn Friday had remained in a heap on his floor all weekend. When she wasn't naked, she had worn a pair of capris and a tank top.

Ellis thought about calling Lindsay and letting her know they hadn't made much progress, but he wasn't up to dealing with her dramatics. Instead, he sent her a quick text. She responded a few minutes later with just an "okay." It didn't seem like she was that concerned about her missing husband.

At loose ends, Ellis sent a quick text to Carter that he had no luck with Bennett and would try again tomorrow. He got a text back that said to call Jack.

Ellis punched in the call to Jack. "Hey, Carter said to call you."

Jack set Patty down in her playpen. "Yeah, I called him earlier and told him I wanted to press charges against your ex-girlfriend for trespassing and battery."

"Lindsay?" When most people mentioned his ex, they meant Lindsay.

"Yeah. She showed up at my office today with her feathers ruffled something fierce. She came into the office, started screaming across the room, then assaulted Olivia. I sent Olivia home shortly thereafter. She didn't want to call the cops, but I did. Lindsay came into my office and assaulted my employee. Carter sent a uniform to the office and took a copy of the security footage and my report."

Ellis grabbed his jacket and his laptop. "Is Olivia okay?"

"She'll have a bruise on her cheek and a fat lip, but otherwise she's fine. We iced her face before I sent her home."

Ellis cursed. "Thanks, Jack. And don't let Olivia talk you out of pressing charges. Lindsay went too far. And Olivia won't be at work tomorrow."

Ellis ended the call and tucked his phone in his pocket. He went straight to Olivia's apartment. It took almost an hour to get there in city traffic. He parked his car near the building, hoping it would be safe for the short time he planned to be there. He planned on packing Olivia up and taking her home with him, whether she liked it or not.

He walked around the building to her door. He pounded on it but wasn't surprised when she didn't answer. He pounded again. "Olivia, it's Ellis. Open up."

Olivia stood on the other side of the door, debating whether to open it or not. Stalling, she called through the door. "I told you I wasn't feeling well."

He banged on it again. "But you omitted why."

Olivia rested her forehead against the door. She figured she had better open it. She knew how stubborn he could be; he'd stand there all night. She unhooked the chain and undid the lock. She opened the door and held it open for him to enter.

Instead of entering the apartment right away, he stopped to cup her chin and tip her face toward the light. His eyes darkened, but he didn't say anything. He eased her back and closed the door behind him. "Why didn't you tell me?"

Olivia glared at him. "Tell you what? That your ex-fiancée doesn't like it that you're sleeping with me, so she punched me? And of course, everyone knows we're sleeping together because that's what you do."

Ellis was momentarily taken aback by her harsh tone. Then he remembered who he was talking to. Olivia had her defenses up, and when they were up, she went on the attack. "Your sleeping with me is not what's bothering you."

Olivia turned her back on him and went back to the couch where she had left her ice pack. Her face still throbbed from where Lindsay had punched her.

"Let me." Ellis took the pack from her and carefully pressed it to her cheek. He couldn't help but feel guilty that it was Lindsay who had done this.

Olivia relented and sat still, closing her eyes. She barely moved when she felt his lips lightly kiss the side of her mouth where her lip was split.

Ellis shifted so that Olivia was resting against him, and he could easily hold the ice to her cheek. He let out a silent sigh of relief when she relaxed against him.

"I feel stupid."

Ellis brushed her hair back from her forehead. "Why?"

She turned her eyes up to his but otherwise didn't move. "I let that skinny little witch punch me. Then she kicked me. And then she smacked me. And surprisingly, she's got a strong arm. Probably all those personal trainers she hires to keep in shape."

Ellis simply tucked her closer. He wasn't going to admit that he had taught Lindsay how to defend herself.

Olivia let herself enjoy the feel of Ellis's arms around her for a few more minutes. "You should probably go."

"Always worried about my car." Ellis kissed the top of her head and removed the ice from her cheek.

Olivia shifted away. "It's a real concern. People in this neighborhood don't see cars like that."

"True." Ellis took the ice pack to the kitchen and put it back in the freezer. "Do you want me to pack you a bag, or do you feel up to doing it?"

Olivia shook her head. "I'm not going home with you. I told you, I don't feel well."

Ellis made the one argument she was sure to listen to. "Come on. You took care of me. Let me return the favor."

Olivia hesitated. "We both have to work tomorrow."

"You don't have to work tomorrow; I told Jack you weren't coming in. And I can work from home. You can lie on my couch, watch soap operas, and just relax."

Olivia smiled at that. "You don't have a TV. I noticed that about you right away."

"Then I guess no soaps. Come on. Let me."

Olivia reluctantly got to her feet. "I take it Jack sent you here."

Ellis followed Olivia to her bedroom. "I sent Carter a text, and he told me to call Jack. That's when Jack told me what happened. I came all on my own. You should have told me."

Olivia went to her closet and pulled out an overnight bag. "I told you I felt stupid. And to make it worse, Jack pulled me off the foundation's security detail on Saturday. I suppose you were right."

Normally, Ellis would savor her admitting that he was right about something, but not this time. "Right about what?"

"I'm not big enough to do security. I thought if I worked out and trained that I could. But the first time someone takes a swing at me, I go down."

Ellis wasn't sure what he was supposed to say to that. So instead of saying anything, he pulled Olivia into his arms. He cupped the back of her head when she pressed her face to his chest.

Olivia took a deep breath and pulled away. "All right. Let me grab a few things from the bathroom, and I'll be ready to go."

Olivia closed her eyes during the drive back to Ellis's house. She was feeling tired and defeated, and not interested in small talk. And since Ellis seemed content to let her be, she simply zoned out.

Ellis carried her bag to his bedroom when they arrived. Olivia followed him. She stripped out of her clothes, tossed them on the floor, and climbed into his bed. She moaned a bit when her head hit the pillow, but otherwise, she was still.

"Want some tea or something?" Ellis tugged off his tie and tossed his jacket on a chair nearby.

"No. I just want to sleep."

Ellis turned off the bedroom light, left the door partly open, and went into the living room so she could rest. He picked up his phone, but there were no messages. After what she had done, he had expected Lindsay to call him, begging him to forgive her and help find her husband. But the phone showed otherwise.

He booted up his computer, intent on working, but couldn't help but take a moment to check his email for any alerts. There was still no activity on Bennett's accounts. It was as if he had dropped off the face of the earth. Or he really was being held captive.

Ellis rubbed his aching chest, unsure of his next move. Given what Lindsay had done, he wanted nothing else to do with her. She had always had a jealous streak. It was that trait that had brought them back together time and again. She never liked it when he dated other women. Their last fight, the one that had ended their on-again, off-again relationship, was about that very trait. Lindsay saw nothing wrong with her stringing along a few men in case their relationship fizzled, but she saw red when he went out with other women. Their last blowup had been a big one, and it had been the last straw, as far as Ellis was concerned. He had simply been tired of Lindsay's drama.

Ellis opened his email and sent all his and Olivia's files on Bennett to Carter. He had told Lindsay to go to the cops, but he had let her talk him out of it. After tonight, Carter could deal with her. He was done.

Ellis looked toward the hall that led to his bedroom.

Olivia was night and day from Lindsay, and not just in looks. Olivia said what she meant, and she didn't play games. When she was mad, you knew it. If she was happy, you knew it. Tonight, he had seen a different side of her, an insecure side. It made him want to wrap his arms around her and protect her.

And he knew without a doubt she wouldn't parade other men in front of him to make him jealous. She was loyal to her friends and cared about them deeply, as he had seen the night of Mrs. Davis's birthday party. She had even come to his side when he was hurt despite their adversarial relationship. She was exactly the type of woman he should have been looking for instead of a Lindsay replacement.

Startled by the realization, he went to the sideboard and poured himself a drink. He emptied the glass and went down the hall. He eased the door open to see her sound asleep. Ellis stripped off his clothes, tossed them on top of hers, and climbed into bed beside her, pulling her to his side.

Chapter Nine

Olivia woke in the early morning, feeling much better than she had when she fell asleep. Ellis was lying on his stomach beside her, one arm draped over her waist, and the other tucked under his pillow. Smiling at the picture he made, she brushed a lock of hair from his forehead. When she brushed a kiss on his mouth, his arm tightened around her.

"I could get used to this," Ellis mumbled, the words brushing against Olivia's lips.

"Oh, yeah?" Olivia kissed him again, sliding her hands under him so she could push him onto his back.

"What man wouldn't want to wake up to a beautiful woman every morning?"

Olivia trailed a few kisses down his chest. "It probably depends on the man."

Ellis rolled over, tucking Olivia beneath him. "And the woman."

"I won't argue with that." Olivia wrapped her arms around Ellis's neck, bringing his mouth to hers.

Ellis obliged, his sudden hunger for her fierce. He grabbed the condom off the nightstand, the one he had optimistically placed there the night before while Olivia was asleep. The taste of Olivia went straight to his head, and he found it difficult to think straight.

Their lovemaking was fast and furious, and afterward,

Olivia lay completely spent beneath him. She admitted to herself that she could get used to falling asleep and waking up in Ellis's arms. She wasn't sure how serious he was when he said it, but it made her feel good to be wanted.

"Such a serious face." Ellis dropped a kiss on her lips before climbing out of bed.

"Just a thoughtful one." Olivia remained on the bed, admiring the view as Ellis went to his dresser to pull out a clean pair of briefs and a pair of jeans.

"Come on, we need a shower." Ellis tugged Olivia with him to the bath.

Half an hour later, they were enjoying a fresh cup of coffee. Olivia sipped hers and simply enjoyed the morning. She supposed she should go to work since she felt fine, but she was feeling too content to move. Instead of the work clothes she had packed, she dressed in a pair of yoga pants and a t-shirt and simply braided her wet hair.

"I meant what I said earlier." Ellis tucked his bare feet under the kitchen chair and leaned forward, his chin resting on his hands.

Olivia focused back on Ellis, tearing herself from her daydream. "Mmm. What?"

Ellis took her free hand and kissed her knuckles. "I said I meant what I said earlier. This is serious. You and me."

His tone had her heart racing. "You think so?"

He kissed her knuckles again. "Definitely. Don't you?"

Olivia had to give him credit. He wasn't shy or insecure. His tone wasn't hesitant, nor was he really asking her if she felt the same; he was stating fact. He knew what he wanted, and it made her heart swell that he wanted her. "Yes, I think this is serious. I just haven't decided what that means yet."

"We can figure that out as we go. But it does mean it's you and me, and no one else."

Olivia nodded. "No one else."

"Good. We'll have breakfast and you can watch me work." Ellis went to the fridge.

"I could die from the excitement." Olivia grinned at his back but stayed in her seat.

They took breakfast to the living room where Ellis booted up his computer and Olivia made herself comfortable on the couch. She had her laptop in her bag but was reluctant to go get it. She was also reluctant to bring up the one topic she didn't want to discuss, but she knew it was necessary.

"What are we going to do about Lindsay and Bennett?" Olivia waited for his answer.

"I already did what I'm going to do about it. I turned everything over to Carter last night." Ellis didn't look up from his computer. As far as he was concerned, he was done with the conversation.

"Do you think it's that simple? Lindsay will be in a rage. And she'll come begging you to help her."

Ellis leaned back and turned his eyes on Olivia. "So what? I agreed to help her because it was the right thing to do. I've known her a long time, and if nothing else, we were friends. But she went too far. She can't attack my girlfriend and expect me to help her."

Olivia was a bit cheered to have him call her his girlfriend, though it seemed an odd choice of words from a man like Ellis. "So we just let the police handle it?"

"Yes, we let the police handle it."

Olivia was quiet for a moment, then asked the question on her mind. "Did you tell Lindsay that?"

Ellis stopped reading his emails and looked over at Olivia again. "Why do you seem to have a problem with this? After what she did yesterday, I figured you'd be doing somersaults at washing your hands of her."

It was more of his washing his hands of Lindsay, more so than her, that would have her doing somersaults. But it didn't seem right to just let the police find Bennett. At the end of the day, Lindsay was still sort of family. Olivia knew Mandy would remain at Lindsay's side until Bennett was found. It didn't seem right to do nothing when family was involved, even hers.

"Just leave it, Olivia. Carter and his partner, Mac, are very competent men. They will find him."

She didn't know Mac, and she had only met Carter briefly. But given that he was married to Selena, and she knew Selena well enough to know she wouldn't marry an incompetent man, she simply nodded and relaxed once again.

Olivia eventually pulled her laptop out and worked a bit. The two of them spent the remainder of the day working out for a short while, showered again but separately, then went out to dinner. Olivia spent the night with Ellis again, and he dropped her off at work the next morning.

The office was quiet. A few people asked her if she felt better, but she had a feeling that she looked pretty happy with herself and already knew the answer.

Olivia had been working for a couple of hours when Mandy showed up. Olivia had seen her come through the office doors and had watched dispassionately as she came to her desk. She knew she shouldn't be surprised by Mandy's appearance; it was inevitable, she supposed. Where one was, the other was sure to follow.

Olivia turned her monitor off and swiveled in her seat to face her half-sister. It was still a shock to see how pregnant she was. "To what do I owe the honor?"

"Always with the smart mouth. You weren't at that dump you call your apartment yesterday, and when I called the office to see if you were in, I was told you took a sick day."

"Since I'm sure you know why I was out yesterday, it makes me wonder what you're doing here."

"Ellis called the cops." Mandy looked around. "Isn't there a place we can talk privately?"

Olivia figured the easiest way to get rid of her sister was to get the conversation over with. "There are rooms."

Olivia took Mandy to a small conference room and closed the door. "If you know Ellis called the cops, why are you here?"

"We told you to leave the cops out of it." Mandy sat, wrapping her arms around the bulk of her stomach.

"And Ellis told you that there would come a time when he had no choice. And trying to protect Bennett from the criminal charges against him will just land the lot of you in jail."

Mandy waved that aside. "Bennett has enough money; he won't see the inside of a prison. His lawyers will have him free before he's even fully processed."

"Not this time."

"Now it will be all over the press. Cops in Hollywood can't keep their mouths shut."

Olivia hoped the press got wind of it. "Then let's just hope that when they do find him, he takes a really pretty mug shot."

Mandy got to her feet. "It isn't funny. The press is going to have a field day. Lindsay is a wreck. She didn't sleep at all last night. She spent the night pacing. And when that didn't calm her, she switched to liquor. She didn't sleep until almost five this morning. And don't think I don't know where you were at five a.m."

Olivia was pretty sure that around five she'd been under Ellis and definitely not sleeping.

Mandy saw the smug smile. "I suppose you think this is funny. Of all the men, you would pick Lindsay's leftovers."

Of all the insults, that one hit its mark. "I think we both know that isn't true. You're just jealous. You never did like him, but part of me always wondered if it wasn't because you wanted him for yourself and couldn't have him."

Mandy's eyes narrowed. "You think you're so smart.

Well, smarty-pants, what are you going to do about Bennett?"

"Nothing. The police have the case now. I'm sure they're at the house now."

Mandy slammed down her purse. "They're tearing apart Lindsay and Bennett's bedroom. They're asking all sorts of horrid questions. When I left, they were headed to Bennett's office and the condo he keeps downtown."

Olivia lowered her tone. "I know it's hard. But the police are better equipped to find him if he's been kidnapped."

"What if he wasn't kidnapped?"

Olivia took her sister's arm and led her to a chair. She looked pale and was rubbing her lower back. "If he's just in hiding, they'll still find him. Do you think he was kidnapped?"

Mandy pulled a tissue from her purse. "How should I know? All I know is Lindsay came back from her honeymoon floating on air. All she could talk about was how much Bennett adored her and how he catered to her every whim. She kept going on and on about how Ellis never treated her the way she deserved."

"I'm not sure what the problem is since you agree with her."

Mandy wiped tears from her eyes. "And you had to go and bring him back into our lives."

Olivia opened her mouth, but no words formed at first. Then she found her voice. "I'm not sure how Lindsay calling Ellis to track down her missing husband has anything to do with me."

"She saw the way he was looking at you during her wedding reception. Everyone there knows you left with him. And what do you think everyone thought the two of you were doing?"

Olivia was getting tired of the conversation. "Lindsay broke up with Ellis. You don't like Ellis. What he and I do is none of your business, or Lindsay's. She lost that right a long time ago."

"Ha. And the minute she crooked her finger, he came rushing to her side. You'll always be second best. Now, what are you going to do about Bennett?"

"I've already told you." Olivia started for the door.

"All right. Wait. Lindsay doesn't trust the police. She thinks that when they find him, they'll arrest him, and she won't get to see him. If you find him first, then she can at least get the chance."

Olivia shook her head. "And if I find him, then the two of them disappear. Not going to happen."

"Look, I promise we'll turn him over as soon as we find him. But we need to see him first. You owe us that much."

Olivia had heard variations on that theme her entire life. Because she came crashing into the family and disturbing it, she somehow was beholden to them. Mandy had always acted like they were doing her a favor by allowing her into their home once a month to visit their father. The odd part was Olivia had always felt that somehow, she was at fault. She was the outsider. She had begged her mother time and again not to make her go visit her dad. But her mother kept telling her he had an obligation to her to see that she grew up well. Olivia had asked her mother why she didn't simply take his money and get out of his life. Her mother had told her he had to take responsibility for his actions. Somehow that seemed to translate to Olivia taking responsibility for her being in their lives.

"All right. I'll keep looking. But I'm not going to help him escape the police. If I find him, I'll call the cops."

Mandy picked up her purse, her eyes now dry. "Fine. I don't think you'll find him, but it will give Lindsay peace of mind that you and Ellis are still looking."

"Not Ellis."

Mandy tucked her purse under her arm and headed for the door. "We both know you'll drag your boyfriend back into this. You haven't got the skills to find Bennett, but I have no doubt Ellis does."

Olivia closed the conference door behind Mandy, needing a moment. Ellis wouldn't be happy with her if he knew she was still looking into Bennett's disappearance. He had seemed well and truly done with Lindsay and the mess she found herself in. But it wouldn't take much work on her part. She already had the trackers in place to find Bennett should he touch any of his bank accounts or investments. The man was used to living in luxury. She doubted he would be able to stay underground much longer. Unless, of course, he had been kidnapped. And if that was the case, the chances of finding him alive after so much time had passed were slim.

* * *

Ellis lay on the lounge chair and watched Olivia in the water. It was early Saturday, and the foundation's charity dinner wasn't until seven. Olivia had spent the night with him, and they'd gotten up early to head to the beach. Olivia claimed she was having beach withdrawals, and he had two choices: he could stay home and let her take his car to the beach, or he could come with her. He'd opted to come with her.

It wasn't exactly a hardship to lie on the lounger and watch her in the water. He'd joined her briefly, but the ache in his shoulder told him he still wasn't fully healed. He didn't want to push his muscles beyond their limits when he had to be at that dinner. This would be the first time he attended as the vice president of Powell Trading, and not Selena's bodyguard. This would also be his first public appearance since the shooting.

But the dinner was hours away, and watching Olivia in the water gave him a whole new perspective of her. She didn't just enjoy the water; she loved it. She lamented the whole way that she should have thought their plans out better. She had a surfboard in her apartment, along with an assortment of beach paraphernalia. Since she didn't have a car, she couldn't drive all her things to the beach. Then she'd complained that his car was too small to hold her surfboard. He'd simply laughed and pointed to the large garage that was off to the side of Selena's house. There was a truck in there that would hold her board and anything else she wanted to drag along.

Olivia spent the next hour in the water before heading back to where Ellis was relaxing. He'd rented the chair and an umbrella so he wouldn't have to sit in the sun. Olivia claimed the chair next to him, wringing the water from her braid.

"Are you doing okay?" Olivia flicked the water from her hands onto Ellis's chest. He had left his t-shirt on, and she wished she had thought of the scars on his chest before she had practically demanded he come. She knew he wasn't going to let her take his car to the beach without him.

"Nothing to lying around and enjoying the fresh air. But I think you're going to need a nap before dinner tonight."

Olivia tried not to pout. She wasn't interested in mingling with L.A.'s rich and not quite famous. She understood why Ellis needed to go. He was one of the city's elite. She forgot sometimes that he worked for one of the largest antiquities companies in the U.S. The company had contracts with people all over the world. And Ellis had told her in confidence that the company also helped stop black market trading of stolen antiquities and artifacts. He was very proud of the work he did, and she couldn't fault him for that. But she hadn't thought about what dating a man like Ellis would mean, or the attention that would be on her when they were out in public together.

"What's the frown for?" Ellis flicked her braid over her

shoulder.

"I was just thinking that I sometimes forget who you really are."

Ellis wasn't sure he was following her train of thought. Not an unusual occurrence. "And just who is that?"

Olivia leaned over and picked up her discarded sundress and pulled it over her bathing suit. "You're Ellis Wallace."

"Okay." Ellis handed her a bottle of water.

She took it, but instead of opening it, she rolled it between her hands. "That means something."

Ellis now had an idea of where this was going. "Is my job going to be a problem for you?"

Olivia turned troubled eyes his way. "Maybe."

"Want me to give up the Porsche?"

She gave him a small laugh, and her mood lightened. "Nah. I like it."

"You like driving it." Ellis took the bottle from her and opened it for her.

"But I'm serious. You're a wealthy man. You're the vice president of a huge company. You make the news. Lindsay is way better suited for a man like you."

Ellis took her hand. "Maybe once upon a time I believed that. And there were plenty of women I dated because they looked good or fit some preconceived notion of the type of woman a man with money and status should date. But none of them came to my house and bullied me into health. None of them made off with my car, hacked my medical records, cooked my meals, or challenged me at every turn. None of them took me to the beach or just spent quiet time with me. You do those things, and I'm beginning to appreciate what I've been missing out on. If you left and didn't come back, I'd miss you."

Tears stung her eyes, but they didn't fall. She instead came to sit next to him on the sand, resting her head on his chest. Her gaze drifted back to the ocean, and she felt nothing but contentment lying next to the man she was in love with. She supposed she had no choice but to figure out how to go about being the type of woman a man like him dated. If she left, she'd more than miss him. She'd be devastated.

Olivia got Ellis into the ocean one last time before they headed out. She had a feeling he agreed to go in with her just so she'd strip out of her sundress again and go back to only wearing her very brief black bikini. She kept it in her workout bag, just in case she had an urge to head to the beach. She'd been known to hit the beach on her lunch break, just to get her feet wet. When the ocean called, she came.

Olivia grinned the entire way back to Ellis's house because he let her drive. It was just a little past two when they arrived. They had plenty of time to shower and dress before they had to leave to go to the dinner. Olivia had her black dress hanging in Ellis's closet and her gold sandals. The dress was the same one she had worn when she'd worked as a bodyguard and was the same one she wore to Lindsay's wedding. She only had one other dress at home, and it wasn't fancy enough for the dinner.

Ellis pulled Olivia into the shower with him, so it was another hour before either of them was ready to get dressed. Ellis watched while Olivia pulled some very fancy underwear out of her bag. He was very much looking forward to peeling her out of her dress later that night. But for now, what he wanted was to see her in his gift.

"I've got a present for you." Ellis came up behind Olivia and kissed the back of her neck. He did it again when she shivered.

"Did you buy me my own Porsche?" Olivia brought her arm around Ellis's neck to hold him close.

"Not this time." His hands drifted over her belly, then cupped her breasts while he continued nibbling on the back of her neck.

Olivia stood helplessly in his arms, struggling to find her words. "Then what?"

Ellis placed one last kiss on her neck and let her go. He headed to his closet and pulled out a garment bag.

Olivia recognized the label on the bag as one from a shop on Rodeo Drive. It was a shop she had never set foot in but knew very well where it was. There was no mistaking it. She took the bag from him and laid it on the bed. She carefully unzipped it. Inside was one of the most stunning dresses she'd ever seen. The dress had two layers. Underneath was a full-length strapless black dress that would hug her figure. Over it was a dark gold lace sheath with cap sleeves and a slightly scooped neckline. The waist was cinched with a belt that matched the lace. It looked like something you might see at a red carpet event.

Ellis took the dress out of the bag the rest of the way. Olivia looked like she was afraid to touch it. "I hope you like it. I told Selena what I wanted, and she helped me pick it out and get the sizing right. She wears lots of white, but I wanted to see you in something different."

Olivia touched the lace with just the tips of her fingers. The lace was soft, and the pattern was unique. "I'm not sure what to say. It's beautiful. But it's too much."

"No, it's not enough. Given all that you've done for me, it's just a token. And I have to admit it's a selfish gift. I want to see you in it."

Olivia took the dress from Ellis and set it down. She turned and wrapped her arms around him.

Ellis was surprised by the hug. They were lovers, but this was different. He held her until she let him go.

Olivia wiped the tears from her eyes, careful to blot them so she wouldn't ruin her makeup. She grinned at him, then turned to the dress. "I'll need help zipping it up."

Ellis helped Olivia into the dress. He zipped it up and then turned her so she could see herself in the mirror. She looked stunning. Her tanned skin glowed against the dark gold, and the upsweep of her hair let the cap sleeves of the dress enhance the slimness of her neck. The bodice enhanced the shape of her breasts and hips, and the rest hugged her body as it fell to the floor. Even without her heels, the dress made her look tall and sleek.

Ellis stood behind her as they both admired the dress, though for different reasons. "I have something else for you, but don't get too excited. I borrowed them from Selena."

Olivia couldn't take her eyes off the dress, so she just nodded. She couldn't believe how well the dress fit her. Once she put on her heels, even the length would be perfect.

Ellis came next to her and set a small black clutch on the bed. Then he opened a box. Inside it were smoky diamond drop earrings that went well with the dress. When Olivia didn't take them from him, he put them in himself.

"There. Now we're ready to go."

Olivia shook her head, but she wasn't sure what she was trying to convey. The earrings probably cost more than her last car, probably her last two. "Selena let you borrow these?"

"She insisted. She sent the earrings and the clutch over with the dress."

Olivia brushed her hands down the length of the dress, then turned to Ellis. "Thank you. It's the best present I've ever gotten."

Ellis heard the sincerity in her voice and was pleased his gift had gone over well. He'd been nervous about giving it to her, unsure if she'd take it from him. With Olivia, he never knew how she'd react. Any other woman would have taken it, even expected it, from him. With Olivia, she had no expectations; she was more comfortable giving than she was taking.

"And I'll have to be sure to thank Selena for her help."

Olivia transferred the essentials from her bag to the borrowed clutch.

Ellis took her arm and led her to the car.

Chapter Ten

"We do want to thank you for all you've done for Ellis. He wouldn't listen to any of us." Theo took a sip of champagne, enjoying an evening out while her daughter was being babysat by her father and stepmother. Since their children were about a year apart, it was nice for the two of them to play together.

Olivia simply smiled at the other women. Selena had grabbed her from Ellis almost immediately after they arrived. The men had also congregated on the other side of the room. She could see John, Jack, and Carter talking to Ellis. Olivia couldn't help but wonder if she was the topic of conversation among that group.

Isabelle seconded it. "Really, we are. Ellis has always been such a big part of The Heart's Way Foundation and has been a good friend. All of us were devastated when he was shot. And it was hard to see him withdrawn and not eating or sleeping well. It's so wonderful to see him back to his old self."

Selena glanced over at Ellis. "I still feel guilty about what happened. And what you've done for him, money can't buy."

Olivia raised a hand to stop them. "I'd say it's been a mutual thing. I only did what anyone else would do. But you three and your husbands are too close to him. He just needed someone on the outside to bully him."

"It worked." Selena took a sip of her champagne and tried

to ignore the ever-present hint of guilt she felt when she looked at Ellis. If it weren't for her, he'd never have been shot. He kept telling her he was only doing what she paid him to do, but it felt hollow after she had seen the reality of what those bullets had done to him.

"Enough. I have to say you look stunning in that dress." Theo waved a hand at the gold and black dress.

Selena gave the ladies a smug smile. "That's because I know what I'm doing."

Olivia touched a hand to the dress, still a bit self-conscious in something so expensive. "I can't thank you enough for helping Ellis pick it out. It's the most beautiful dress I've ever owned."

"Don't let him fool you. He did most of the work. I helped with the size, but he knew exactly what he wanted to see you in tonight. When he called and said you were no longer going to do security for the party but were coming as his date, he asked for my help. And he paid extra to have the hem altered. One thing he knows his way around is the female form."

Theo giggled into her glass of champagne. "I bet he does."

Isabelle couldn't stifle her accompanying laugh. "None of us knows from personal experience, but I'd bet money on it. Well, none of us knows, except for Olivia."

Olivia blushed as three pairs of eyes filled with feminine curiosity turned her way. "I don't kiss and tell."

Isabelle nodded, satisfied that they knew the answer. "That blush says it all. I wore that same look after John and I became lovers. Theo and Selena had that same look, too."

"I just adore Jack. More so since we had Patty. There's nothing like watching our little girl wrap that big, strong man around her tiny finger."

Isabelle cleared her throat. "Speaking of your little girl, there's something I wanted to tell all of you. We were going to wait a little longer, but John sort of spilled the beans to Theo. John and I are pregnant."

The only one who didn't know was Selena, and she was the first to grab Isabelle and give her a big hug. "I'm so excited! We get to have another shower. But I thought you two were going to wait."

Isabelle shrugged. "We were. But I've spent so much time playing with Patty that I decided it was time. John was willing to oblige."

"I bet he was." Theo took her turn to congratulate and hug Isabelle.

Olivia, not terribly used to displays of affection, gave Isabelle a quick hug. "If your child grows up with even a small part of your big heart, the world will be a better place."

Isabelle's eyes teared up. "That's the sweetest thing anyone has said to me since I found out I was pregnant. John and I are blessed, and we hope to share that with our child. And we hope to teach him or her how important it is to be a part of something bigger than yourself."

The conversation drifted from babies to the foundation, then to their respective men. Olivia was about to excuse herself and go see if Ellis was hungry when a man joined them.

"Mac. It's good to see you. We weren't sure if you were going to make it." Selena hugged the large, blond-haired man.

Olivia realized who this was. Ellis had told her about Carter's partner.

Selena gestured to Olivia. "Mac, meet Olivia Knight. She's a friend of Ellis."

Mac gave the woman a once over. "I hear it's a bit more than that. It's nice to meet you."

Olivia took the hand that was extended to her. "It's nice to meet you, Detective. Ellis mentioned you were Carter's partner."

"Yes. And I know it's not the most appropriate time, but I'd like to speak to you about a certain matter."

The three women all turned curious eyes to Olivia. Olivia ignored their looks. "Why don't we chat outside?"

Mac took Olivia's elbow and guided her to the terrace. The ocean in the distance could still be heard over the noise from the party. "I know you are aware Carter and I are looking into Bennett Roger's disappearance. Ellis assured me he was handing the case over to the police and stepping out of it. Does Ellis know you're still tracking Bennett?"

Olivia figured she could answer the question in one of two ways. She could be coy and refuse to directly answer the question, or she could admit it. But she had no desire to be arrested for interfering in a police investigation. "We did turn everything over. I just wish we could have helped more."

Mac wasn't buying it. "Your fingerprints are all over his accounts. We both know it."

"But can you prove it?" Olivia took a step back, intimidated by the detective's size as he loomed over her.

"Look, Miss Knight, I can appreciate you're trying to help a friend. But interfering in a police investigation is a serious offense. I'm giving you until morning."

Olivia gave up the ruse. "Mandy came to me and asked me to help. Lindsay is upset, and rightfully so. Mandy is her best friend. My entire family is with her during this time. I have the skills to track him digitally if he surfaces at all. There have been no ransom demands; no one has stepped forward, and he has yet to be found. It's not against the law for a private citizen to help out family."

"Maybe not. But you're still interfering. And from what I hear, Lindsay isn't going to be happy you're still involved. Jack is pressing charges for trespassing, and I'm told you'll be pressing charges for assault. Makes me question your motive. Maybe you're not helping the search but hindering it."

Olivia had forgotten Jack was pressing formal charges against Lindsay. It hardly seemed worth the effort. A good attorney would get her off, given the nature of the circumstances behind the attack. "The assault, as you call it, was nothing more than a jealous ex-girlfriend lashing out. She was upset when she found out I was seeing Ellis. It isn't worth pursuing."

"Be that as it may, we both know Lindsay won't be happy to find out you are still trying to find her husband. The LAPD doesn't need your help, and neither do I. I meant what I said. If I find out you're withholding evidence or had any part in his disappearance, I will arrest you." Mac started to walk away when he spotted Ellis headed their way. He turned back to Olivia.

Olivia shook her head at Mac. "He doesn't know."

Mac strode forward and spoke to Ellis on his way back inside. "Do yourself a favor and get a rein on your girlfriend. If I find out she's involved in any way, I will arrest her."

Ellis watched in confusion as Mac strode away. Mac had been particularly tense lately, and tonight was no different. Ellis let the man go and turned to Olivia. "What was that all about?"

Olivia tried to shrug it off but failed. She had to admit Mac intimidated her. There was something quite fierce about the detective. Selena, Theo, and Isabelle seemed to like him, but he had shown her a different side of himself.

Ellis turned back to see Mac speaking to Jack and John, then left. Ellis had a feeling he knew why Mac had sought Olivia out. "You're still looking into Bennett's disappearance, aren't you?"

Olivia nodded. "Mandy came to me and convinced me not to drop the case. You have to understand how close Mandy and Lindsay are. Mandy is worried about her friend."

Ellis had to bite his cheek to keep from saying what he

really wanted to say. "I am well aware of what Mandy is like. She was a constant fixture during my relationship with Lindsay. They spent more time together than Lindsay and I did."

Olivia took a step toward Ellis, but there was no softness in his gaze as he watched her. "Do you think Mac knows I'm the one looking into Bennett's accounts?"

"Does he know? Yes. Does he have proof? Not likely. You're too good for that. Why did you lie to me?"

"I knew you'd be upset. Lindsay reacted out of pure emotion, not any other reason. Her husband is missing and has been for too long. We both know that under normal circumstances this never would have happened. Lindsay is normally even-tempered. Mandy came to the office and pleaded with me."

Ellis rubbed a hand over his face. "Mac was serious about arresting you. We should get back. This night certainly hasn't gone quite the way I'd planned."

"Look, Ellis, I'm sorry. I wasn't going to keep digging, but Mandy came to me, and I couldn't say no. She said Lindsay didn't trust the police to find him, and if they did, they would just arrest him. She said the police were tearing apart Lindsay and Bennett's bedroom and turning my father's house inside out."

"It will be worse in the morning. His disappearance made the news tonight. Carter told me just a little while ago. You can't shield your family from the circus that's about to start. And I imagine I'll have a few reporters camped on my doorstep asking me how I feel about my ex-fiancée's husband's disappearance."

Olivia hadn't thought about that. Both Ellis and Bennett were public figures. The press would easily find out about Lindsay's past relationship with Ellis. Lindsay had wanted fame and fortune, and it looked like she was getting it, but Olivia doubted anyone could have anticipated what would happen when she married a Hollywood producer.

Olivia and Ellis bid everyone goodnight. Selena had asked if everything was all right, and they both assured her it was. Selena would know her husband was investigating Bennett's disappearance. Carter would have told her.

They were halfway back to Ellis's house when Olivia spoke. "I did it for Mandy. She has always had a knack for making me feel guilty. She always felt I was an intruder in the family and made sure to remind me every chance she got when I was younger. I can't say I blame her. If my mother had come home one day with another child and forced him or her into our lives, I can't say I wouldn't have been resentful. And given her feelings for Lindsay, not helping would hurt Mandy, not Lindsay."

"I'm not upset you are helping your sister's friend. I'm upset you lied about it. I thought today on the beach we had a connection. I don't like being lied to, and I don't like that I had to hear it from someone else."

Olivia hadn't thought about it from his point of view, but he had a point. She should have told him. "I am sorry."

Ellis just kept driving. When his phone rang, he ignored

it. It had been ringing on and off for the past hour.

Olivia picked up his cell and the number was Lindsay's. "It's your ex."

Ellis glanced at the phone in Olivia's hand but dismissed it. "I already know what she wants. I'm guessing the press is outside your father's house."

Olivia hated that Lindsay felt she could call Ellis and have him come running to her at any time. "You might as well go. She'll just keep hounding you."

Ellis ignored her comment. "I should take you back to your apartment. We'll pick up your stuff, and I'll drop you off."

Olivia felt her heart sink to her stomach. She knew he was upset with her, but she hadn't realized how much. Instead of arguing with him, her pride kicked in, and she shut her mouth.

When they arrived at Selena's estate, there were no people, press, or paparazzi waiting outside, which Ellis could only be grateful for. His address would be a little harder for people to find, but it wasn't impossible. The gated estate would afford him some privacy, but he didn't like that people would be camped outside Selena's gates. Selena and Carter wouldn't be too pleased about it either, but they would be more worried about him than themselves. It had not been a pleasant feeling having the woman he had protected for the past six years turn the tables on him and make it her mission to protect him.

Olivia didn't say anything as she carefully eased herself

out of the car, careful not to snag the dress. She headed straight for Ellis's bedroom and contorted her arm until she could grab the zipper of the dress. Standing in her fancy underwear, she hung up the dress and zipped it back into the garment bag it came in.

Ellis slowly followed. He was upset she hadn't told him she was still digging into Bennett's disappearance, but he was more worried about getting her away from him. Though the press might find out she was the sister of Lindsay's friend, it was unlikely they would seek Olivia out unless she was seen with him. He wanted to make sure that didn't happen.

"I'll grab my things." Olivia went to her overnight bag and pulled out a pair of jeans. She tugged them on and then grabbed a t-shirt, not wanting to be undressed for any longer than necessary. Within two minutes she had everything packed up, with Selena's earrings on the dresser and her new dress tucked under her arm. She was tempted to toss it back at him, but her heart ached too much to start a confrontation over the dress.

Ellis led her back to his car. He tucked her bag in the backseat, but Olivia kept the dress, folding it in her lap. They remained silent until they reached Olivia's apartment.

"I'm not any happier about this than you are." Ellis turned troubled eyes her way.

Olivia climbed out of the car, tugging her bag from behind the seat. When Ellis went to open his door, she stopped him. "I don't need your help. Goodbye, Ellis."

Ellis watched as Olivia half ran the distance to the

apartment building. He rubbed the ache in his chest, but it didn't have anything to do with the healing bullet wounds. He hadn't liked the way she said goodbye. Instead of following her, he left the parking lot and headed back to the estate.

Olivia stopped inside the door of the apartment, watching Ellis as he drove away. She wiped at the tears that fell now that he was gone. Hadn't she told herself he would hurt her? And hadn't she known deep down Lindsay would come between them, one way or another? This wasn't quite how she had envisioned the end of her relationship with Ellis, but she supposed there wasn't a good way to envision it.

Once inside her apartment, she went to the bedroom and hung up her dress in the back of the closet. Maybe one day she'd find the courage to wear it again, but she couldn't imagine that time. She then tossed her bag in the closet after pulling her laptop out. She went to her desk and booted it up. She knew sleep would elude her and figured she would get out of Bennett's accounts before Mac made good on his threat to arrest her for interfering.

Olivia had been online for an hour and was about to shut down her last tracker when one of her alerts triggered. Numbly she pulled up the alert. One of Bennett's smaller accounts had been accessed at a motel outside of town. It certainly wasn't the type of place a man like Bennett would spend the night. Since she was still dressed, she figured it couldn't hurt to check it out. She called a cab and waited outside until it arrived. The rude driver dropped her off at the motel, made a snide comment about women of the night, leered at her, and drove off instead of waiting as she'd asked.

Olivia looked around the parking lot, wondering what had possessed her to come out in the middle of the night to chase electronic tracks. She was about to call for a cab when she saw a familiar car. Lindsay drove a flashy pink Corvette, though Olivia was surprised she would drive it into this neighborhood. And honestly, she was surprised Lindsay knew this neighborhood existed. Lindsay had grown up in a modest, middle-class household, but she had gotten used to the life of a rich girl when she had met Mandy.

Olivia dug into her bag and pulled out her camera. Her classes in private investigation said that documenting everything was essential. Olivia discreetly hid behind a light pole and took pictures of Lindsay's car, the surrounding parking lot, the hotel sign, and the doors of the rooms Lindsay might be occupying.

Wishing she had a car, Olivia did her best to stay in the shadows. Several people came and went, and Olivia took pictures in case any of them were of interest. Most of them looked shady, and not the type of people Lindsay would hang out with or even know.

After a couple of hours, there was little activity. She supposed she needed to think this through next time. By the time hints of the sun started peeking through the clouds on the horizon, she was hungry and needed the bathroom. She was getting ready to call it a night when another familiar car pulled into the parking lot. Heart pounding, she pulled out her camera again. First, she took a picture of the vehicle and the man who stepped out. Then she saw one of the doors on the second floor open to reveal Lindsay wearing a thin nightgown trimmed in lace. Olivia's heart broke when she snapped a picture of Lindsay throwing herself into Ellis's arms right before the motel door closed behind the couple.

Chapter Eleven

"I can live without the theatrics, Lindsay." Ellis pulled her arms off his shoulders and not-so-gently pushed her down to sit on the bed.

Lindsay broke down in tears. "I don't know what else to do. The police have been all over, asking all sorts of awful questions. You're my friend. I need you."

And wasn't that how most of their conversations started? Ellis never realized how one-sided their relationship had been since the beginning. Had they still been a couple the past couple of months, she would have been useless while he was recuperating. She wouldn't have wanted to listen to him talk about what had happened. She wouldn't have been there to take care of him. She would have paid someone else to do it. She wouldn't have pushed and bullied him into health.

"I'm here. But there is nothing else I can do. You have to let the police do their job. Carter and Mac are friends."

Lindsay planted her hands on his chest. "What if I were the one missing? You wouldn't just give up on finding me."

Ellis stood still, feeling nothing at the touch of her hands on his chest. "You're not the one missing. And I don't like the way you treated Olivia."

Lindsay dropped her hands. "I shouldn't have hit her. I know that. I was jealous. I have no other excuse."

Ellis crossed the room and took a seat on the edge of the

second bed. "You married another man. You gave up any right to feel jealous. We're finished."

Lindsay shook her head and came to kneel at Ellis's feet. "I made a mistake. I don't love Bennett. I love you."

Ellis looked down into Lindsay's wet eyes. "I don't love you anymore, Lindsay. Not like I used to."

Lindsay dropped her head. Her voice was a whisper. "You can't mean that."

Ellis remained silent. He knew coming here was a mistake. But when he'd gotten home, he had found an email in his inbox from an anonymous sender. It showed a picture of Bennett on a beach, sipping a cocktail, and flirting with a pretty waitress. He was guessing the picture was taken somewhere in Mexico, where local authorities weren't likely to follow.

"Come on. You need to rest. You probably haven't slept in days." Ellis lifted Lindsay by her forearms.

Lindsay took the opportunity to once again throw herself against him. She kissed him, desperate for the response she had always been able to elicit from him.

Ellis didn't respond to the kiss but let her cling to him until she realized it. There had been a time when he would have given anything for Lindsay to come to him like this, desperate and wanting. But now he felt nothing, not even the tiniest stirring of desire.

Lindsay eventually let go. "You love her, don't you?"

Ellis nodded and led Lindsay back to the other bed. He gently tucked her under the covers. "Yes, I love her. But right now, I have a feeling she thinks I broke up with her."

Lindsay tucked the covers under her chin. "Why?"

"The press will release Bennett's disappearance on the morning news. I want her as far away from this as possible. The press is going to have a field day. I suppose your calling me here did both of us a favor. It will give us time to figure out what we're going to do."

"I guess I'll play the grieving wife."

Ellis wasn't sure he liked the role of love-sick ex-boyfriend helping out an old girlfriend, but he supposed he didn't have much of a choice. That would be how the press portrayed him. And if it kept Olivia out of the news, then he would do it. "We'll have to arrange a press conference after the story breaks. You'll need to get Mandy, your brother, and anyone else close to Bennett together. We can say I'm helping the police find your husband. The police will hold their press conference and discuss any progress they've made in finding him."

Lindsay's eyes drifted shut, but she didn't fall asleep. "They haven't made any progress. No one knows where he went. I might not love him, but we made an agreement. I have to find him."

Ellis didn't ask what that agreement was. He supposed it had something to do with playing the dutiful wife while she spent his money. "They will. If Bennett were to go into hiding, where would he go?"

Lindsay's eyes opened, her confusion plain. "What do you mean? He was kidnapped."

"Maybe. I'm not convinced. The fact that he's wanted by the LAPD for a hit-and-run makes me skeptical."

Lindsay went to argue with him, then stopped. "Why would he fake a kidnapping?"

Ellis rubbed his tired eyes. "I'm not saying he did. But if he did, where would he go?"

Lindsay thought about it and turned to face him from the bed. "He could be in France. He has a house there. He could be in Italy. A friend of his owns a hotel there, and he goes there when he wants to get away from the pressures of his job. We honeymooned there."

A fancy hotel in Italy probably wouldn't have fancy drinks and waitresses on the beach, but he pulled out his tablet and wrote down the name of the hotel Lindsay gave him anyway. Then he took down his address in France. It was a place to start, and there was no telling if that picture sent to him was current or old. "We should sleep."

"You'll stay?" Lindsay snuggled down.

"Might as well. It's almost morning. And I don't want the press to wait outside Selena's estate. Once we make our statement, the press should leave you alone." Ellis kicked off his shoes and lay on top of the other bed.

"I am glad you're here. And I'm sorry for what I did to Olivia."

Ellis closed his eyes. "You can tell her that the next time you see her."

The room was quiet for a little while. Then Lindsay spoke. "We really are over, aren't we?"

"Yes, Lindsay. We are."

An hour later, there was a loud pounding on the door. Ellis rose and grabbed his jacket. He had a license to carry the gun he had tucked there. He put a finger to his lips for Lindsay to keep quiet. He went to the door and peeked through the peephole. He swore and opened the door.

Mac and Carter swore and lowered their weapons. Mac was the one who spoke. "Should I even ask what you're doing here?"

Carter entered the room and looked around to make sure there was no one else there. He glanced at the woman lying on the bed. He recognized Lindsay from when they had searched her bedroom. "Has anyone else been here?"

Ellis set his weapon on the dresser. "No. Why?"

Mac holstered his gun and gave Lindsay a cold look. "Because your girlfriend here used her husband's credit card to pay for the room."

"This was a waste." Carter pulled out his comm device and radioed their status to headquarters.

Lindsay sat up, letting the blanket drop, completely oblivious to the fact that her nightgown was practically see-through. "I'm sorry. I didn't think of it when I booked the room. I just didn't want anyone to be able to trace me here."

"Like who?" Carter ignored the view.

Lindsay eyed the man. "I don't know. The kidnappers or something. Living with Ellis taught me to be cautious."

Ellis pulled his phone out of his pocket and pulled up his email. "I think it's a safe bet that there are no kidnappers waiting in the wings to grab you."

Mac, too, ignored Lindsay. Ellis's tone caught the man's attention. "What is it?"

Ellis handed Mac his phone. "I got this late last night, right after Lindsay called me. I'm fairly certain Bennett was not kidnapped."

Lindsay climbed out of bed and snatched the phone from Mac. Her angry cry could be heard down the hall. "How dare he! He made me think he was kidnapped, and instead, he's living it up on the beach."

Carter took the phone from her to get a look. "It certainly looks that way. But why send this to Ellis?"

Ellis took his phone back and forwarded the email to Mac's and Carter's email. "This whole situation is fishy. First Lindsay gets an email showing her husband tied up, but no ransom was made. And if this photo is to be believed, he's somewhere on a beach enjoying himself. If Bennett just wanted to disappear so he wouldn't be arrested, why the games?"

Mac didn't care. "Hollywood is a funny place. Maybe he thought he could use a kidnapping story to gain sympathy from the public. Or maybe he thought it would get a judge to let him off lightly."

Ellis didn't buy it. "He has a lot of money, and we both know he will end up paying off the family of the woman he hit. The family will take the payout because it's better than the spectacle of a trial. Then he'll play the sympathetic character to the press, of how he really needs help and is willing to do whatever it takes to make amends. Then he plays it up big, gets probation, and his next film will be a huge success."

Mac had lived in L.A. long enough to know Ellis's scenario rang true. "Okay, so why is he in hiding? If nothing else, there should have been a ransom demand by now if he's trying to make the kidnapping look authentic. People have noticed his disappearance. We've been talking to people he knows, friends, and colleagues. If it's a charade, it's gone on long enough."

Carter tossed Lindsay the robe that lay on a nearby chair. "I say Lindsay gets dressed, we all go to the station, and figure out our next move. We'll play it as a kidnapping to the press for now until we can trace him. Then when we find him, we can arrest him for faking his kidnapping right after we book him for the hit-and-run."

The three men waited outside while Lindsay got dressed.

"So, what are you doing here?" Carter leaned against the building.

"That's the question I keep asking myself."

Mac answered. "Women. They do have a way of working their way under your skin. The question you should be asking yourself is how you're going to explain this to your other girlfriend."

Ellis tucked his hands in his pockets. "What are you talking about?"

"The pretty blonde. Personally, I'd take her over the piece of work in that motel room. Less drama. Except for when you get near her again. Who do you think called us?"

Ellis straightened. "Olivia called you?"

"She said she didn't want to be arrested for obstruction and said she had been shutting off her trackers when she saw the charge to the motel room. She said theoretically she was turning trackers off on the accounts. She's not stupid. She knew we were also watching his accounts, so she called to let us know not to bother coming here, that it was just you and Lindsay in the room. We had to be sure, of course, and came anyway."

Ellis realized Olivia had pulled the address from where the charge came from, and she must have seen him arrive. Knowing there was probably not an explanation on the planet she would believe, he felt his heart drop to his stomach. She would never believe he had come here with nothing but an altruistic motive. She would think the worst. And he couldn't blame her.

* * *

Olivia swore she wasn't going to watch the news, but she couldn't seem to stop herself. Lindsay wore black, and with her dark hair and skin tone, it was very dramatic. Mandy stood by her side, her arm wrapped around her best friend's waist. Ellis stood in the background, along with a host of other people. Olivia wasn't surprised to see her father and stepmother there showing their support. Baxter sat in a wheelchair off to the side. Baxter didn't need the wheelchair, but since he was so wobbly on his feet, he preferred it in public. As for the rest of the people, she figured they were friends and family of Bennett's. They all stood far off to the side, just standing there, supposedly in support of Bennett's distraught wife.

Olivia was torn between wanting to scream and cry as she watched the press conference. Instead, she went back to her laptop once the first round of questions was over. She had removed the rest of the trackers. She had sent a text to Mandy, who wasn't happy, but Olivia wasn't about to push Detective Quinlan. She had a feeling the detective would have made good on his promise and shown up on her doorstep and charged her with interference or obstruction. Either of those charges would prevent her from ever getting her investigator's license. Though right now, she wasn't sure she even cared.

Olivia wanted to believe that Ellis had gone to that hotel room for no other reason than to talk some sense into Lindsay. Had he shown up at the hotel room of any other woman, she would have given him the benefit of the doubt. But this was Lindsay, his first love. Ellis hadn't said those words to her. They hadn't made any promises to each other. He had spoken words of caring and a future at the beach, but it was hard to remember those words with the image of Lindsay, barely dressed, flinging herself into Ellis's arms. He hadn't exactly fought her off.

Cursing her suspicious nature, Olivia turned her attention to Ellis's accounts. They had been working together long enough that she knew how to easily access his computer. Within twenty minutes, she was in Ellis's email account. She didn't see anything out of the ordinary in his inbox. Feeling only slightly guilty, she checked his outgoing. She found an email he sent to the police. She opened the file and saw the anonymous message and the picture of Bennett on the beach, flirting with a waitress. So much for being kidnapped.

Olivia sat back and blindly stared at the picture. The timestamp on the email he received was before Ellis went to Lindsay's hotel room. Twenty minutes later, Olivia had Ellis's text messages. Lindsay had sent him a text right after she checked into the hotel. Ellis hadn't left until after he had received the email, hours after the text. Knowing he went after he'd seen the email made Olivia feel a little better but no less suspicious.

Olivia looked back at the picture. She had seen pictures of this resort before. Lindsay and Mandy were forever booking vacations and getaways together. Maybe she could locate the resort from old pictures. Hacking into Mandy's computer might take too long, so going to the source was her quickest option. Mandy didn't bother to password her computer, claiming that passwords were such a hassle.

Instead of sulking around her apartment, she got dressed and headed over to her father's house. Mandy would have pictures. And since everyone would be busy with the press conference for a while yet, she should be able to get in and out without having to confront her family.

Olivia nodded to the housekeeper when she arrived, but otherwise, no one else was home. Olivia went to Mandy's room. As expected, the laptop was out in the open and turned on. Like most people, she kept her pictures stored in the default folder location. Mandy was organized, and the pictures she was looking for were easy to find. There was one particular hotel in Cancún that they loved. Olivia pulled out her flash drive and copied the files.

Olivia was about to put the computer back to sleep when a notification popped up. Curious, Olivia clicked on it. She quickly put the flash drive back into the computer and started copying emails. The email was from the same anonymous sender who had sent the picture of Bennett to Ellis. Why would Mandy get emails from the so-called kidnapper?

Olivia didn't want to waste a lot of time, so she simply dumped the rest of Mandy's files on the drive. She made copies of all incoming and outgoing emails. Olivia wasn't sure what was going on, but she was going to find out.

Olivia had paid the cab driver to wait, so she simply slipped back out of the house. Olivia figured she had a couple of options. She could go to the police, or she could go to Ellis. Now that she wasn't running strictly on emotion, she started to think clearly again. She knew Ellis was upset with her about lying, but she was starting to wonder if his dumping her at her apartment hadn't been him trying to keep her away from the press conference. He must have realized last night at the charity dinner that he would have to make an appearance. Shaking her head, Olivia decided on option three and went to the office. She could use the computer network there to dig into the mystery emailer. She would worry about her relationship with Ellis later.

Three hours later, she had more questions than answers. She went to the vending machine and grabbed a snack. On her way back, she spotted Lindsay coming through the office doors.

Olivia tossed her granola bar on the desk and locked her computer screen. "How did you get in?"

Lindsay grabbed the chair from the cubicle next to Olivia's and took a seat. "Security let me in. I told him I came to pick you up and give you a ride home. I don't know how I knew you'd be here on a Sunday, but I just did."

"That answers the how. My next question is why?"

"I didn't want to go home. Mandy wasn't feeling well and wanted to rest, but I just couldn't face my empty bedroom."

A bit perplexed, Olivia took a seat. "So you came to see me instead?"

Lindsay crushed the black fabric of her skirt in her hands. "I owe you an apology. And I guess I owe Jack one, too. I shouldn't have attacked you. I'd like to chalk it up to stress, but it was plain jealousy. I guess, because of our history, I think of Ellis as mine. The other women he dates I can ignore because I don't know them. I couldn't ignore you."

"I'm not sure I heard an apology in there."

Lindsay laughed at that. "You always were difficult. I am sorry. I guess I finally burned my bridges with Ellis."

Olivia leaned back and folded her arms across her chest. "I saw you with him last night. Are you sorry for that, too?"

Startled, Lindsay dropped her purse. "What do you mean you saw us?"

Olivia gritted her teeth to keep from yelling. "Mandy asked me to keep tracking Bennett's accounts. I saw the charge at the hotel, saw your car, and decided to stake it out. Imagine my surprise when Ellis showed up."

"Oh, Olivia, it wasn't what you think. I admit I wanted what you were thinking, but he didn't. Last night I realized he doesn't love me anymore. He loves you."

Olivia wasn't ready to pour her heart out to the other woman, but she wasn't ready to dismiss her either. "Are you telling me you threw yourself at him, and he turned you down?"

Lindsay dropped her head. "I even got a little grabby, and he didn't respond even a little. When I kissed him, I knew it was truly over."

Olivia didn't like the image of Lindsay kissing Ellis, and she would be confronting Ellis with that fact when she saw him again, but she supposed she understood Lindsay's desperation. Her entire life was in upheaval. And given what Olivia had found, things were only going to get more complicated.

"All right. I accept your apology. And as long as you promise to keep your hands off him in the future, I won't do something nasty to your computer."

Lindsay rose and grabbed her purse where she dropped it.

"It's a deal. I definitely don't need you doing something to my computer, and I've no doubt you could. I guess I should go."

"You can do me a favor. You can drive me to Ellis's and drop me off. There's something I want to show him."

Lindsay nodded. She waited while Olivia grabbed her laptop, and then she drove her to Ellis's, leaving Olivia at the gate.

Chapter Twelve

Olivia made herself comfortable in the kitchen while she waited for Ellis. She wasn't sure where he was, but she wasn't worried. She knew where he wasn't, and he wasn't with Lindsay. She made herself a late lunch and settled at the kitchen table. The anonymous email had come from a server in Cancún. The email itself had been blank, with no message inside. The only thing it contained was the subject line, and it simply said, "Done yet?" About an hour ago, an email had gone back out from Mandy's email that said, "Not yet."

Other than Mandy emailing an unknown person in Mexico, Olivia didn't find anything else. She had dug into Mandy's cell phone records and found several text messages over the last couple of months between Bennett and Mandy, but she only had the cell numbers and times, not the actual messages. She had nothing incriminating. It would take longer to get the actual messages, and she wasn't sure she wanted to risk getting caught hacking into Mandy's messages since the police most likely were tracking everyone in the family's phones.

For good measure, Olivia checked Baxter's phone records, but there were no calls or texts between the two men. Lindsay's brother wasn't exactly the friendly type. There were hardly any calls on his phone at all, not even from his wife. Olivia felt slightly guilty doing the same thing to her father and stepmother, but their phones were mostly clean. There had been a few incoming and outgoing messages and calls to Bennett over the past couple of months, but nothing that raised warning flags.

So what could Mandy have to do with Bennett's so-called kidnapping? Had Mandy gotten the ransom demand? It didn't seem likely, but the kidnapper might know that Mandy would do anything for Lindsay. And if that was the case, the kidnapper knew both women well.

But that scenario didn't play for her. But neither did Mandy kidnapping Bennett. So Olivia was back to the question of how Mandy was involved.

Olivia opened an email software program and anonymously forwarded the emails between Mandy and the unknown person to Mac and Carter. They would suspect it came from her, but she wasn't going to make it easy for them to prove it. Olivia did keep her trackers off Bennett's accounts but placed a few discreet ones on Mandy's phone and email. They wouldn't be obvious to someone looking, but unfortunately, they wouldn't be overly helpful. They would just alert her to any activity.

Her next step was the photos. Mandy loved to take pictures and loved to take pictures of herself and Lindsay. Olivia would be embarrassed if she had that many pictures of herself floating around out there for people to find, but she didn't think Mandy and Lindsay had the same hang-ups that she did.

Olivia hadn't gotten through even half of the first folder

of photos when she heard the front door alarm signal Ellis's return. She glanced at the clock on the computer. It was already after nine. She had lost a few hours going through Mandy's files.

Ellis rubbed his tired eyes but then stopped only a few steps into the house. Though the alarm had been set, he hadn't left the light on in the kitchen. He doubted Selena or Carter were waiting for him, so that left one person. His heartbeat increased a little as he headed to the kitchen. There Olivia sat, bent over her laptop at the kitchen table.

"You look like hell, Ellis. When's the last time you slept?" Olivia folded her hands on the table and gave Ellis a once-over.

"I could ask you the same question. What are you doing here?" Ellis wanted to snatch her up and drag her to the bedroom, but he instead went to the cabinet to grab a glass. His mouth was so dry he was surprised he could speak. He'd spent the morning and afternoon fielding questions, then he'd decided to remain at the police station and see if he could be of any use. He hadn't wanted to come back to his empty house. He'd gotten used to having Olivia around.

"Waiting for you." Olivia closed the screen of her laptop.

"I told you I didn't want you here."

"I'm not gotten rid of that easily. And be honest, you're happy I'm here."

Ellis grunted and swallowed the entire glass of water.

Olivia glared at him in response to his grunt. "Seriously, are we going to go back to the beginning? Do you want me to be annoying and obnoxious?"

Ellis leaned back against the counter. It was taking all his willpower to keep his hands to himself. "And what do you call showing up at my place uninvited, if not a return to the beginning?"

"I suppose you have a point. But if you wanted to keep me out, you should have changed the codes. Not that that would have stopped me for long. But seriously, when's the last time you slept? Your body is still healing, whether you want to admit it or not."

Ellis yawned and answered. "I don't know. Probably over thirty-six hours, minus a brief nap. Now it will be even longer since I have to drive you home."

Olivia crossed her arms over her chest. "Forget it. I'm not going anywhere. I appreciate the sentiment, but I'm not interested. You won't be able to keep our relationship out of the press. I don't know why you want to even try."

Ellis scowled at her. "I can keep it out of the press if there isn't one."

Olivia crossed to where Ellis stood. "Okay. I can accommodate you under one condition. Look me in the eye and tell me you slept with Lindsay last night in that hotel room."

Ellis opened his mouth, but no words came out. He couldn't look down into Olivia's bright blue eyes and lie to her. And it wasn't in him to hurt her that way. "Can't you see that it's better if you go home? At least until we find Bennett. Reporters in L.A. can be brutal. I spent the entire morning playing word games so the press wouldn't get a juicy scandal out of Bennett's disappearance. I could tell they wanted me to play the jealous ex or give something away that would incriminate me in his disappearance. They'll hound you if they see us together."

Olivia stood on tiptoe and wrapped her arms around Ellis's neck. "I love that you want to protect me. But that's not what couples do. We should be there for each other, support each other. And despite whatever it is you're thinking, I can take care of myself, and I'm not going to pretend that I don't care about you."

Ellis's arms came around Olivia's waist. "It could get ugly."

"I don't plan to leave your house until we figure out what happened to Bennett. And since I don't have any clothes here anymore, we either solve it fast before I need a change of clothes, or we spend most of the time naked in your bed. Your choice."

Ellis shook his head but gave up. "I'll take option two. I'm too tired to solve this case before you need to change clothes."

Olivia kissed him, pulled back, then kissed him again. "I like your choice, though I think you might be too tired for option two."

"You might be right." Ellis took her hand and led her back to his bedroom. He quickly stripped both Olivia and himself.

Olivia stopped him before he grabbed her. "Seriously

though, I don't have a change of clothes. I'm going to toss these in the washer first."

Ellis watched half in surprise and half in amusement as Olivia gathered up her clothes and went to put them in the washer. His body was exhausted, so he climbed under the covers to wait for her. He was probably making a mistake not taking her home, but he didn't have the heart. And since he didn't want her to go, it was hard to make himself say what needed to be said or do what needed to be done to make her leave.

Olivia strolled back into his bedroom. "I should make you beg. You have no idea how I felt when I saw you go into that hotel room with Lindsay."

Ellis sat up. "I know exactly how you felt. It's how I would have felt if I had seen you walk into the hotel room of an ex-boyfriend. I would have wanted to tear the man apart."

"It hurt, Ellis. A lot."

Ellis tossed the covers aside, no longer tired. Her eyes were wet as she looked at him, her naked body trembling slightly. He gathered her against him, lightly stroking her hair as he held her. "I'm so sorry, Olivia."

"If you weren't recovering from gunshot wounds, I'd punch you."

Ellis laughed and picked her up. He then carefully set her on the bed. "I like it better when you're soft and loving."

Olivia leaned on her elbows so she could enjoy the view. "As opposed to being argumentative and hard-headed?"

Ellis came down on top of her. "I like to think of you as feisty. But right now, I want the other side of you."

Olivia pulled his mouth to hers and opened her thighs to him. "I can be soft and loving."

Ellis kissed her deeply while he slowly penetrated her body. He had no words to tell her how he felt. When he'd told Lindsay he was in love with Olivia, it was the first time he'd realized it. But his love for Olivia was so much bigger than what he'd felt for Lindsay that the words wouldn't come. He felt his throat constrict on anything he might say to her. So instead, he kissed her deeply again, slowly rocking back and forth inside her until her nails were digging into his back, her hips straining against his.

Olivia couldn't speak, could barely breathe, while Ellis made love to her. All she could do was cling to him. When her body climaxed beneath him, her heart became forever his.

Ellis didn't want to stop, but his body wouldn't let him continue, and he followed her over the edge. He collapsed on top of her, completely drained.

Olivia pushed until Ellis rolled over onto his back. She felt the stickiness between her thighs and sighed. She supposed making love without protection wasn't the smartest move, but she couldn't regret it. She wouldn't have given up the last few moments for anything. She went to the bathroom and washed up. When she came back, Ellis was staring at her from the bed.

"Are you going to say it, or should I?" Olivia stood in the

doorway.

"I suppose I should. It shouldn't be so hard."

Olivia shook her head. "It should be hard when it matters. It shouldn't be easy."

"Come here." Ellis held a hand out to her.

Olivia came and sat on the bed, taking Ellis's hand in hers. "Well?"

Ellis sat up and cupped Olivia's cheek. "I love you, Olivia."

Tears welled up in her eyes, and she leaned forward to kiss him. Her lips were still pressed to his when she spoke. "I love you too."

Ellis's hands slid under her hair, cradling her head. He wasn't sure how long they sat that way on the bed, but Ellis didn't want to let her go.

Olivia eventually broke off the kiss, her breathing unsteady. She pushed Ellis back down. Then she slipped under the covers and laid her head on his chest. "Don't ever send me away again."

Ellis's fingers stroked her spine. "I don't think I could if I tried."

Olivia kissed his chest, snuggled down, and went to sleep, happy that she was back where she belonged.

* * *

Olivia woke before Ellis, but that didn't surprise her. He needed to rest. And Olivia's mind was racing from what she'd discovered yesterday, and her thoughts wouldn't let her sleep any longer. She grabbed a t-shirt from Ellis's dresser before heading to the kitchen. She needed coffee, then she needed to get to work. The quicker they figured out where Bennett was, the better off their relationship would be. Olivia knew Ellis was concerned, but she wasn't going into hiding.

Olivia pulled up the images she had been going through last night. She knew somewhere in here she was going to find some photographs that would tell her where Bennett was hiding out. As she went through them, she began to notice a pattern. She found the photos she had been looking for and had the name of the resort that matched the picture of Bennett. She wasn't as interested in Bennett's probable location as she was in what she was seeing.

"Such a frown for a Monday morning." Ellis dropped a kiss on Olivia's head before heading to the coffee pot.

"I think you need to call Jack. Get a man ready to head down to Mexico. Then you need to call Lindsay."

That stopped Ellis mid-pour. "You want me to call Lindsay?"

Olivia stretched her shoulders, keeping her eyes on the screen. "You'll need her permission to send Jack's man to Mexico. I was going through some photographs taken last year when Lindsay and Mandy went there. They vacation together a couple of times a year, and when I saw the photo of Bennett on the beach, I recognized some of the hotel's landscape in the background."

Ellis finished pouring his coffee and came to stand behind Olivia. "I'm not even going to ask how you know about the photo of Bennett. It will just tick me off, and I'm feeling too good this morning to let you ruin my mood."

"Good. It's better that you don't. But seriously, you need to call Lindsay and get her to authorize the charges."

Ellis massaged the tension from Olivia's shoulders. She'd been trying to work out the kinks since he'd entered the kitchen. "I can call her. What's the name of the resort?"

Olivia pulled up the resort's website. Then she leaned into Ellis's hands. "You can call Lindsay while I take a shower."

Ellis shook his head and headed for his phone while Olivia headed to his bath. He heard the loud buzzer of his dryer, so he figured she'd timed it so that her clothes would be dry by the time she finished. He made the call to Lindsay. She was distraught to find out her husband was hiding at her favorite resort in Mexico, but Ellis ignored her tears and varied complaints. He also asked a few questions about Mandy and how she could be involved. That upset Lindsay even more, so he simply hung up without asking any more questions. He then sent a quick email to Jack to get a man down there to find out if Bennett was there. With that done, he headed to join Olivia in the shower.

Olivia made room for Ellis when she heard the shower door open. The shower was more than big enough to hold both of them. And his shower didn't run out of hot water like hers did.

"How did she take it?" Olivia asked while she rinsed the shampoo from her hair.

"Probably how you think she would. She saw the picture yesterday, so she won't be surprised if Jack's man finds him. She wants answers, and she's willing to pay whatever amount it takes to get them."

Olivia ran conditioner through her hair before handing Ellis the bottle of shampoo behind her. "I think Jack's man will find him. But Bennett's disappearance isn't what interests me anymore."

"No?" Ellis soaped up a wash rag and began rubbing it over Olivia's body.

Olivia shivered under the hot spray when Ellis's hands replaced the rag. "No, it's not. But it isn't what you're doing either that has my interest."

Feigning hurt, Ellis backed Olivia up against the wall of the shower. "I think I can change your mind."

Olivia wrapped her arms around Ellis's neck and let Ellis lift her against him. She completely lost track of what she was going to say.

A little while later, satisfied and satiated, Ellis turned off the taps and carried a limp Olivia to his bedroom and dumped her on the bed, uncaring of the water seeping into his blankets and sheets. "So what has you more interested than Bennett's disappearance?"

Olivia sat up, pushing her wet hair out of her face. "I don't know why I let you distract me."

Ellis turned his head to see Olivia grinning at him. "It

must be love."

Olivia came to stand behind Ellis and placed a kiss on his shoulder. "Must be. And I hate to be the voice of reason, but that's the second time you've made love to me in less than twenty-four hours without protection."

Ellis turned to face her. "That's the second time you've let me."

Olivia touched her fingers to the scars on his chest. Every time she saw them, it came home to her that she almost missed being with him like this. He could have been killed, and she never would have known how much she could love him. "Then there is that. I know you said you love me. And I do love you. But we're taking a pretty big risk. Maybe it's not the kind either of us should be taking right now."

Ellis was quiet for a moment, but just a moment. "I can't figure you out. I can't decide if that's a good thing or a bad thing."

"What does that have to do with risk?"

Ellis shrugged. "Nothing. It's just what came to mind in response to what you said. If you don't want to risk getting pregnant, I can understand and respect that. It's something we should talk about before doing."

"Probably. We'll make a deal. Next time we use protection until we sort this all out. And if I'm pregnant, you have to marry me."

Ellis's knee-jerk response surprised both of them. "How about you marry me anyway, and if you are pregnant, we'll worry about it then."

Olivia opened her mouth, but no words came. She stood there trying to formulate a response, but Ellis spoke before she could find her words.

"It's not that far out in left field, you know. It's what people do when they're in love. And you're already practically living here."

"Okay."

Ellis was about to argue but realized she had answered in the positive. "You're saying yes?"

Olivia threw herself into his arms and almost knocked him back a step. She kissed him, then let him go just as quickly as she grabbed him. "I have to snatch you up before someone else does."

Ellis gave her a wary look. "You don't mean Lindsay, do you?"

That stopped Olivia in her tracks. She had been going to grab a towel. It was a little awkward to have this conversation while dripping water on the carpet. "No, I didn't mean Lindsay. But I suppose I should tell you that she and I had a little woman-to-woman chat about you."

"Do I want to know what you two said?"

"I threatened her, and she agreed to leave you alone. You loved her once. It's not something you or I can just forget."

"You once loved another man. We both have a history. The only difference is that your husband is gone, and his presence can't come between us. I did love Lindsay once, but I don't anymore."

"Are you sure? Because I'm pretty sure that if you and I

weren't together, you would have spent the night with Lindsay in that hotel room, and it wouldn't have been in separate beds."

Ellis slowly shook his head. "No, I wouldn't have. I'm the one who broke off our on-again, off-again relationship five years ago. I was getting tired of the games. She didn't want to commit to me, but she liked having me around. I wasn't good enough to marry ten years ago, and five years ago she wouldn't even commit to keeping our relationship exclusive. I played the fool long enough, and that was the end of it. Lindsay and I have been over for a long time. She hasn't been anything more than a friend for years. And she wasn't exactly a good friend, either."

"You're a good man, Ellis. I don't think she appreciated that." Olivia left the room to grab a towel but immediately came back.

Ellis watched as Olivia dried her hair, then pulled his t-shirt back on. "We're engaged, and you could be pregnant, and all you have to say is that I'm a good guy?"

Olivia tossed Ellis the towel. "You should dry off and get dressed. And being a good guy is a good thing. I was married to a not good guy, so I would know. I know I can marry you and that you're not going to turn into some other person. I knew I could really care about you when you threatened to have me arrested."

Ellis rubbed the towel over his wet hair, then toweled off the rest of the moisture on his skin. He got dressed and followed her back to the kitchen. "You care to explain that?

I was mean to you, so you knew you could care for me?"

Olivia poured them both a fresh cup of coffee. "When I first met you, I didn't trust your charm. It put every instinct I had on high alert. When you were hurt and rude to me, I couldn't stay away."

Ellis took the cup she held out to him. "So if I had been rude to you when we met, you wouldn't have kept me at a distance?"

"Yep." Olivia sat back down behind her laptop.

"I meant what I said earlier. I don't understand you sometimes." Ellis took the chair beside her.

"Good. Then you won't get bored after we're married."

"You and boring don't belong in the same sentence."

Olivia leaned over and kissed him. Then she became all business. "We can discuss marriage later. I think I might know who kidnapped Bennett."

Ellis sipped his coffee. "I thought we established that Bennett wasn't kidnapped."

"No, but I think he might have been manipulated. Sort of the same thing in this case."

"I don't think I'm following your train of thought." Ellis slid over to see her screen. On it were tons of pictures of Lindsay.

Olivia enlarged a few of the photos. "What do these pictures have in common?"

"They're all of Lindsay."

"Yes. But they have something else in common." Olivia pulled up a few more.

Ellis looked at the photos, but he didn't see anything odd about them. "I don't get it."

"They were all taken by Mandy."

Ellis still wasn't following. "Like you said, Lindsay and Mandy go on vacation together every year."

"Ellis, all of these photos were taken by Mandy. Mandy is also corresponding with your mystery email sender."

Ellis looked up in surprise. "You hacked Mandy's email? Are you sure she's emailing our mystery man?"

"I hacked your email yesterday and I found the picture you sent Mac and Carter. I recognized the location from the vacation photos Mandy had shown the family. She loves to show off her vacation photos. While I was downloading her pictures from her laptop, I saw an email notification come through, so I dumped all her emails. I think she and Bennett organized his disappearance. And I think I know why."

Ellis wasn't going to discount Olivia's theory. She knew Mandy better than he did. When she had been around while he was dating Lindsay, he did his best to ignore her. "Ok, why?"

"Mandy is in love with Lindsay. I found this photo. You can tell it's photoshopped, and it tells a clear story."

Ellis looked at the photo. He was pretty sure those were his arms around Lindsay. But instead of his head and body, Mandy's body overlaid his. It looked like the two women were kissing.

"I don't know what Mandy said or did to get Bennett to pretend to be kidnapped, but I'm guessing Bennett is our mystery emailer. The email that came in wasn't incriminating, but it was certainly suspicious. The emailer asked if Mandy was done yet, and Mandy said not yet."

"So Mandy got rid of Lindsay's husband in such a way that Lindsay would rely on her best friend for comfort." Ellis closed the laptop lid. He didn't want to look at the photo any longer.

"Except that Lindsay didn't go to her best friend. She called her ex-boyfriend instead, the man Mandy would have seen as a rival for Lindsay's affection all these years."

Ellis still had a hard time believing what that picture implied. "But Mandy married Baxter and she's expecting a baby. Why marry another man when you're in love with your best friend?"

"It is her best friend's brother. Makes an odd kind of sense. Mandy gets to be closer to Lindsay through marriage. Now they're family."

"That kind of makes it creepier." Ellis wasn't entirely sure he bought into that part of Olivia's theory.

"Sort of, I guess. But I say we have Jack's man confront Bennett. Then we can confront Mandy. Lindsay is going to be hurt by this, but it's better that it comes out now. Mandy wouldn't hurt Lindsay for the world, but Lindsay should know Mandy conspired with her husband."

Ellis picked up his phone and sent Jack a text. Jack answered a few minutes later. Ellis then turned to Olivia. "Either way, Jack has a man headed to the airport today. The flight is a short one, and it shouldn't take long for Jack's man to find Bennett. By tomorrow, Lindsay will have her answers. Let's just hope she can live with them."

Chapter Thirteen

Ellis and Olivia were sleeping when Ellis's phone rang. Olivia stirred but just buried her face in Ellis's chest. Ellis grabbed the phone.

"It's Lindsay." Ellis turned on the bedside lamp.

"I'm getting tired of her midnight calls." Olivia buried her nose in the pillow when Ellis sat up.

"What's up, Lindsay?"

Olivia couldn't hear what Lindsay was saying, but her voice sounded as if she was yelling into the phone.

Ellis swore. "All right. Give us an hour."

"Don't tell me. We're headed to Lindsay's."

"Mandy disappeared."

Olivia pushed her hair out of her face, squinting against the light of the lamp. "I'll get my laptop. Mandy isn't tech savvy. She's probably got a paper trail a mile wide."

Ellis got up and pulled on some clothes. He picked up Olivia's clothes and tossed them to her. "We should also make a stop at your apartment."

Olivia made a face at the pair of underwear Ellis tossed at her. "Yeah, we should do that. A lady needs more than one pair."

"We can spend the weekend packing up your apartment. It's silly to keep it."

Olivia pulled on her clothes, sans the underwear. "You mean you don't want to move into my apartment?"

Ellis gave her a dirty look. "Think of the Porsche."

Olivia laughed at him. "I am thinking of the Porsche. Why do you think I agreed to marry you?"

Ellis tossed a pillow at her. "I think we'll need to write it into our vows that you will not steal my car."

"Now there is a promise I can't keep. And think of poor Mrs. Davis. I can take her out in style."

Ellis kissed her roughly and pulled her with him to the kitchen where her laptop was. "We will have to get you a car, though. I can't keep chauffeuring you around. Selena is going to start wondering why she's paying me."

"Jack, too."

"We'll expense your time to Lindsay's account. Seems only fair since she keeps pulling us out of bed."

"Just promise me one thing. If I am pregnant, we won't buy a minivan. I don't think my heart could take it."

Ellis just laughed at her while he pulled on his shoes and waited for Olivia to check Mandy's accounts.

Olivia booted up her computer and started searching. "There's no activity on Mandy's email or her bank accounts. Maybe she's driving somewhere."

"Let's just hope she hasn't gotten theatrical and headed for the border."

Olivia grabbed her bag and put the laptop inside. "If she is, she'll have to stop for gas eventually."

They drove to Olivia's father's house, but Lindsay was the only one awake. She let the pair in.

Lindsay wiped at the tears that streamed down her cheeks. "We had a terrible fight. I asked her why she would conspire with my husband to pretend to be kidnapped. She denied it at first, then admitted to it when I pressed her. She said I knew why. Then she said it was all Baxter's fault, which made even less sense. I asked Baxter what Mandy meant, but he said he didn't know. Then he just went to bed like he couldn't care less that Mandy took off. She's pregnant. She's not thinking clearly."

Olivia looked at Ellis, but he made no move toward Lindsay. Olivia took her hand and gently pulled her down onto the sofa. "I think Mandy is upset because of your marriage. I don't know why Bennett agreed to disappear, but I think I know why Mandy wanted him to."

"Why?" Lindsay took the tissue that Ellis handed her.

"I think Mandy is in love with you."

"Of course she is. She has been for years. What does that have to do with Bennett being in Mexico?"

Olivia was taken aback by Lindsay's candid admission that she knew Mandy was in love with her. "Did you two ever act on it?"

"Don't be silly. I'm not in love with Mandy. I'm in love with Ellis."

Ellis ignored the second part of Lindsay's words. "We think she convinced Bennett to leave and fake his kidnapping. We think she wanted you to think he was kidnapped so that you would lean on her for comfort."

Lindsay looked at Ellis, then Olivia. "Mandy wouldn't do that."

Olivia disagreed. "We think she did. She hates Ellis and

did everything she could to split the two of you up. There's no reason to think she wouldn't do the same with Bennett. And since Bennett was already in hot water with the police, he probably figured heading to Mexico was a way out. But his sending that picture to Ellis put an end to the ruse and forced Mandy to change her plans. Now Bennett simply stays in hiding to avoid prosecution. Mandy probably panicked when you confronted her."

Lindsay looked at Ellis, who nodded. Then she looked back at Olivia. "Can you find her? What if she does something drastic?"

"Like what?" Olivia felt her stomach clench.

"She said she couldn't live without me any longer; then she stormed out. I tried to stop her, but she got in her car and tore out of the driveway. What if she hurts herself?"

Olivia pulled out her laptop to see if there had been any activity. So far, nothing.

Ellis pulled out his cell phone. "I'll let Mac and Carter know what happened. They can have the police be on the lookout for her car."

Lindsay began to cry in earnest, and Olivia held her until her tears were spent.

The three of them remained in the living room while Olivia waited to see if she would get a hit on Mandy's accounts. The sun was coming up when Ellis's phone rang.

"Hello?"

Olivia and Lindsay sat on the sofa trying to listen in on Ellis's call. With a brief "we'll be there," Ellis hung up.

"That was Mac. They found Mandy. She's fine but in police custody at the hospital. She tried to jump off an overpass. Mac said she's distraught and asking for Lindsay."

Lindsay got up and grabbed her purse and keys. "I'll be right there."

Ellis stepped in front of her. He looked at Olivia, who nodded. "We'll take you. You shouldn't be driving."

Olivia glanced up the stairs. "Should I wake Baxter?"

Lindsay's response was quick. "No. He would just upset her more. They had a big fight yesterday, too, but I don't know about what."

Ellis drove them to the hospital. Olivia climbed into the back seat and let Lindsay sit in the front. When they got to the hospital, they had to pass through security.

Carter saw them and waved them through. "She's pretty upset. The doctor had to give her some meds to calm her down. She wants to talk to Lindsay."

Carter led them to the room, but only Lindsay was allowed to go to her side.

Olivia and Ellis stood outside the entryway but could see Mandy in the bed.

"You came." Mandy held her hand out to Lindsay.

"Of course, I did. We're friends. But why did you and Bennett pretend Bennett was kidnapped?"

"I thought that if I could get rid of Bennett, it would be just you and me again."

Lindsay took Mandy's hand. "But it's not just you and me. You married Baxter and you're having a baby. Why did you do that if you hadn't gotten over me?"

Mandy yanked at her handcuffed wrist, suddenly angry. "It's all Baxter's fault. He said I owed him for getting rid of Ellis. He wanted me and said it was pointless for me to keep pining over you. But I refused to marry him. Then he promised to help me get rid of Bennett if I married him. But you married Bennett anyway. Then Baxter said if I had his baby, he would find a way to permanently get rid of Bennett. But then Bennett hit that woman, and Baxter said he had a better idea. He and Bennett came up with the idea that Bennett should pretend to be kidnapped. That way he could get out of the country before he could be arrested, and I'd have you all to myself again."

"Oh, Mandy. I don't love you like you love me."

Mandy turned to where she could see Ellis and spat the words at him. "No, you love him. But now he doesn't love you."

Carter led Olivia and Ellis to where Mac waited. An officer was keeping an eye on Mandy, and Carter had heard enough.

Mac handed Ellis and Olivia a cup of coffee from the vending machine. "Mandy will have to stay. She'll probably be kept over for a psychiatric evaluation. And as far as I can tell, there isn't much we can charge Baxter or Mandy with. Bennett wasn't kidnapped. We can charge Baxter and Mandy for withholding their knowledge of Bennett's whereabouts, but no one made Bennett go."

Olivia leaned against Ellis. "I think it's sad. Baxter

manipulated Mandy into marrying him, playing on her feelings for his sister. Lindsay didn't care that her continued friendship with Mandy led her to believe there could be a future between them. And what will happen to her baby? She doesn't seem fit to raise it, and Baxter isn't the best role model. It's so messed up."

Ellis pulled Olivia closer to his side. "As Mac said, no one made Bennett go, and Mandy needs help. You can't fix this."

Olivia looked at the two detectives. "What will happen to Bennett?"

Mac responded. "Depends on if he returns or not. If he comes back to the U.S., he'll be arrested for the original criminal charges, then face charges for faking his kidnapping. Otherwise, it will take time to extradite him. Our people are tracing the IP address from where that email came from. My guess is you'll eventually tie it to Bennett."

"Me?" Olivia's eyebrows rose at Mac's words.

Mac gave her a genuine smile. "I figure you'll be faster than our guys. And this time I won't threaten to arrest you for it."

"Appreciate it." Olivia shook the hand Mac offered her.

Ellis shook both men's hands. "Thanks. I think I'll take Olivia home. It's been a long night."

Ellis took Olivia first to her apartment so she could pack up enough clothes for the week. Olivia had texted Jack letting him know she wouldn't be in the office. He texted back that his man found Bennett. Since Jack had already emailed Carter and Mac about his whereabouts, there was nothing else for her to do.

Back at Ellis's house, Ellis fixed them a light breakfast. Olivia sat at the counter watching Ellis scramble eggs. "Did that seem a bit anticlimactic to you?"

Ellis set a plate in front of Olivia. "Nope. No one got shot, and the police will work on getting Bennett back to the U.S. to face charges. Lindsay will probably get a quickie divorce, and Mandy will be all right, though she'll probably divorce Baxter."

"Can't say I blame her. I never liked Baxter."

Ellis scooped up some eggs and transferred them to Olivia's plate. "You already know how I feel about him. But he didn't do anything illegal. He just made some suggestions. Mandy is the one who was corresponding with him via email and is the one who will have to face the consequences. We have no proof that Baxter knows where Bennett is."

"What if I found some?"

Ellis almost dropped his plate. "Stay out of it, Olivia. It's over."

"You heard Mac; he says it's okay if I trace the email. It wouldn't be anything to drop some extra tracking tags on Baxter. Now that the police have found Mandy and know where Bennett is, he might think it's safe to contact Bennett."

"You're assuming he is in on the plan. Nothing in what Mandy said to Lindsay makes me think Baxter was anything more than a manipulator."

Olivia bit her lip, then spoke. "Okay. I'm going to do it anyway."

Ellis took a bite of his eggs. "I know. Thanks for being truthful about it."

Olivia finished her eggs. "I'm exhausted. What do you think about skipping packing this weekend and spending it at the beach?"

"How about we spend Saturday packing up your apartment and spend Sunday at the beach?"

"Ever practical. Okay, but you have to promise we'll get to spend all day Sunday at the beach."

Ellis put her plate in the dishwasher and led her to the bedroom. "It's a deal."

* * *

"That's quite a story. And that was good work, by the way." Jack took a bite of his sandwich while talking to Olivia.

Olivia took a bite of her salad. Jack had called her into the office and bought her lunch. "I feel bad for Mandy. She has a loser husband, is having his baby, and is in love with her best friend who doesn't love her."

"Don't bother to feel sorry for her. Heartbreak can be survived. She needs to move on and stop pining away for what she can't have."

"I traced the email back to Bennett. He's still cozied up on the beach in Mexico, but something tells me he won't be back to face the music unless forced. I sent the information to Mac and Carter, but at this point, all they can do is file it away until he's back on U.S. soil."

"Anything on Baxter?" Jack handed Olivia a napkin.

"At first, no. There wasn't much activity on Baxter's phone at all. I had gone back over his phone records and not much popped. But I know Baxter. He has that cell phone with him at all times. Since Mandy married him, she has been complaining about how he's always calling her, asking her to do one thing or another for him. It got old listening to her complain. But if Baxter is always calling her, why are there no calls on his phone?"

"I take it you found a second phone."

Olivia pulled up her findings. "I sure did."

Jack looked at her notes. "Doesn't change the fact that Mandy knew where Bennett was. But it sort of makes sense. Bennett disappeared without a second thought, and he probably couldn't care less about his wife or her best friend. Just turn over what you have to the cops. I assume the second phone has some calls coming and going from Mexico."

"And on Bennett's real phone, not a burner. At this point, Bennett probably knows the cops know he wasn't kidnapped. Baxter or Mandy probably told him. I promised Lindsay I would get her the info so she could get divorce papers served. It will probably take forever to gain her freedom, but she'll get it eventually."

"Still going for your investigator's license?" Jack tossed the wrapper from his sandwich in the trash.

"No. Ellis is really worried about me moving to the front

lines. And since we're getting married, I figure I can let it go."

Jack swallowed his bite and coughed on it. "Married? When did that happen?"

Olivia took another bite of her salad. "Just this week. I figured I should tell you because I'll be requesting time off soon. I'm letting Ellis tell Selena, but she'll be ecstatic and probably offer to give him a month off. But I don't plan on doing anything elaborate for the wedding, so it will probably be sooner rather than later."

"Congratulations. We all like Ellis. Guess we don't have to worry about him being depressed anymore."

Olivia smiled to herself. "Nope. I should get back to work. I'll email Carter and Mac about Baxter."

Olivia got a text message from Selena about an hour later, so she knew Ellis told her. She received a congratulations email from Mac, so she knew Selena had told Carter. When she got a text message from Isabelle sending her congrats, along with the date of her upcoming baby shower, she figured the announcement had completed the rounds.

Figuring it was probably best she let her family know, she called her stepmother Regina first. Regina warned her about rushing into anything, and then said she hoped she was happy. Olivia hung up, knowing she would break the news to her father, and then it would make its way to Lindsay and Mandy.

Olivia called her mother next, and her reaction was what she expected. Her ever-practical mother told her to make sure she signed a prenup and to let her know when the wedding was so she could attend. Olivia didn't bother to tell her mother that Ellis was disgustingly wealthy. She'd break that news to her after the wedding.

When Olivia's phone rang later in the day, she answered it when she saw it was from Ellis. "Told your family yet?"

Ellis leaned back in his chair. "Yes. My mother has threatened bodily harm if she doesn't get to help plan it. Believe me when I say it's easier to let her help than to fight her off. She's persistent. My two brothers just said congrats and hoped I knew what I was doing."

Olivia was a little nervous about meeting Ellis's family, but it would be a little while yet before that happened. "I told Jack, Regina, and my mom. I say we elope. The thought of my mother and father in a room together is enough to give me chills."

Something in her tone had him asking, "You're serious, aren't you?"

"You can bet your car on it. What do you think?"

"I think I can find a beach to whisk you off to without anyone being the wiser."

Olivia felt heat gathering in the pit of her stomach at the thought of her and Ellis on a private beach somewhere with no family or friends for miles. "It's a date."

"I'll pick you up after work, and we can get started on the details."

Olivia looked at her calendar. "I need to go to my apartment first. Since I have a ground-floor apartment, a friend of Mrs. Davis wants to take over my lease. I need to sign some papers for my landlord tonight. Why don't you pick me up there?"

"That was fast."

"When I told Mrs. Davis last night that we were getting married, she asked about the apartment. I called my landlord this morning and told him I had a taker for the space, and he agreed to let me out of my lease early. Her friend already came by today to see the space and wants it."

"All right, I can pick you up there. You can get an early start on packing."

They spoke for a few moments longer and hung up. Olivia finished catching up on some of the work she had missed yesterday and packed up her bag and laptop. She caught the bus at the stop that was near the office.

She stopped first at the landlord's office and signed the papers. She checked her mail, then went to her apartment. The door was open, and she frowned. It would figure that her landlord would forget to lock her door on his way out. He was notoriously scatterbrained.

She closed the door and was about to lock it when she realized she wasn't alone. She turned to see Baxter sitting on her couch.

"You just couldn't leave it alone, could you?" Baxter's harsh words filled the small space.

Olivia tensed but didn't try to run. "You always were selfish. I wondered what you had said to Mandy that convinced her to marry you. You exploited her feelings for your sister."

"Don't bother feeling sorry for her. She used me as much as I used her. I was tired of sleeping alone, and Mandy owed me. I thought about going for you, but you're used goods."

Olivia ignored his remark. "Owed you for what?"

"For getting rid of Ellis. My dear sister couldn't bear to see me angry with her. She dropped Ellis because of how upset it made me to see her with him."

Olivia kept her back against her front door. "I knew you were a jerk, but I never knew you were crazy. Mandy thought you were going to get rid of Bennett for her."

Baxter got to his feet. "She is gullible. But in the end, it was easy enough to convince Bennett to disappear. When he hit that woman, he gave me the perfect way to get rid of him. I hadn't cared one way or the other, but Mandy kept nagging me. And as her pregnancy progressed, she got worse. Kept saying how I promised her. I was ready to pay someone to take him out when he conveniently agreed to disappear. But now I have cops knocking on my door, claiming conspiracy to commit fraud, or some such nonsense. I have you to thank for that. Mandy is in the hospital swearing she'll divorce me. I have you to thank for that, too."

"You should have covered your tracks better. And the punishment you get won't be nearly as much as you deserve."

Baxter let out a shout and came at her.

Olivia went for the door when Baxter lunged for her, but she underestimated his speed, and he rammed her into the door before she could get it open. He let out a satisfactory grunt when her elbow jammed into his midsection, but he didn't let go of her.

"I should beat you within an inch of your life. Who do you think you are?"

Olivia managed to hook a leg around Baxter's and knocked him to the floor. Unfortunately, he got a grip on her shirt and managed to take her with him.

Baxter grabbed her hair and brought his fist up. "You'll regret tangling with me."

Olivia managed to get free and dodged his fist. Instead of hitting her in the face, he hit her arm. She felt her arm go numb from the strength of his punch but managed to stumble away from him. She opened her front door and was about to let out a scream when she saw Ellis running her way.

Ellis brought her up against him when she threw herself at him.

"Baxter is in my apartment."

Ellis set her to the side and yanked the door open. "Big mistake."

Olivia watched as Baxter got back on his feet and took a swing at Ellis. But Ellis was faster, and Baxter was at a disadvantage since he had a difficult time standing. While he was strong enough to attack someone much smaller than him, he was no match for Ellis.

Olivia grabbed Ellis's arm when he would have slammed a fist into Baxter's face. "I called Mac and Carter, and they're on their way. You don't want to mess up his ugly face."

Ellis nodded, but then redirected his fist to the man's gut. "That's for touching my woman."

Baxter coughed and lay on the floor. It was a minute before he could get to his feet. He looked like he was going to attack Ellis again, but then thought better of it and remained where he was.

Ellis stood over him until Mac and Carter arrived.

Olivia turned to see the two men heading their way. "That was fast."

Ellis kept his eyes on Baxter. "I called them when my computer pinged and told me Baxter was on the move. I realized he was headed your way. I tried to call you, but I got your voicemail. I called Carter for backup."

Olivia took her phone out of her bag and saw several missed calls from Ellis. "I shut the ringer off while I was at work. I forgot to turn it back on."

Carter glanced past Olivia and saw Baxter on the floor. "Ellis's instincts are always spot on. He said Baxter had a vengeful streak."

Olivia glanced back at Mac, who had his weapon drawn but was facing it down against his thigh.

Carter cuffed and read Baxter his rights while Mac holstered his weapon and came to take Olivia's statement. He wrote down what she said word for word. "You'll need to come in and sign your statement, but it can wait until morning. No reason to let this guy out on bail any sooner than necessary."

Ellis pulled Olivia against him while they watched Mac

head to the squad car where Carter was waiting. He then pushed her inside the apartment, closed the door, and backed her up against it.

Olivia responded to his rough kiss. Both of them were breathing heavily when he released her.

"I'm going to see to it that you get some serious self-defense lessons. I was scared to death that Baxter might have hurt you."

Olivia wrapped her arms around Ellis's waist. "You don't need to worry about it. I've had enough excitement working my first case as an investigator that it will be my last. I'm going back to my computer."

Ellis looked down into her eyes and saw the sincerity there. "You mean that?"

"Yes. I already told Jack, right before I told him we were getting married. I'm sure he's secretly pleased."

Ellis swept Olivia up in his arms and carried her to her bed. "I love you, Olivia. I want you to be happy."

Olivia brushed a lock of hair from his forehead. "I am happy. Being an investigator seemed a lot more exciting than spending the rest of my life behind a computer. But I've found something better. I'm marrying the man I love; what more could I want?"

Ellis kissed her tenderly, but the kisses quickly became heated. He stripped them both. It was almost an hour later before either of them moved.

Olivia kissed his chest. "We should probably get dressed. I don't trust leaving your Porsche out there any longer than necessary."

Ellis rolled off of her. "I'm not worried about the car."

Olivia leaned over to kiss him but wasn't surprised when he instead got out of bed and got both of them redressed and on their way back to his house, despite his words.

Hours later, when both of them were once again naked and spent, Ellis spoke in the darkness of his bedroom. Ellis pulled Olivia against him and spoke softly in her ear. "You're getting those self-defense lessons."

Olivia grinned in the darkness, her heart filled with happiness. That was probably the most romantic thing he could have said to her. She simply said, "Yes, dear."

"You better hurry up; the rest of our guests are due any minute," Ellis shouted up the stairs.

Olivia shouted back that she'd be there in a minute and smoothed out the skirt of her dress. They were throwing a housewarming party and invited all their friends and family. Her mother was in town and was already downstairs, probably driving Ellis crazy. Her mother had insisted on helping plan the party and had arrived early to help since she hadn't been able to plan a wedding reception. Ellis's mom was also downstairs helping with the preparations. His brothers were watching the women work. Olivia was just happy she didn't have to do anything and was happy to let her mother and new mother-in-law take over.

She heard the doorbell ring and decided to take pity on her husband and come help answer the door. Within the hour, the house was full of family and friends. John and Isabelle had shown up first, Isabelle's stomach now proclaiming she was indeed pregnant. Jack and Theo showed up next, with little Patty eager to get out of her car seat and play. Carter and Selena were a little later than usual, but they claimed they were still in their honeymoon phase and entitled to be late.

Olivia circled her new living room and spotted Mac, who was chatting with Mrs. Davis. Mrs. Davis seemed extremely fascinated by the pictures he was showing her. Olivia had found out that Mac had two children, and she was sure Mac was showing her their pictures.

Ellis came up behind Olivia and placed an arm around her waist. "I'd say the party is a success."

"Definitely. We may never get them to leave." Olivia leaned against her husband.

Ellis tipped up her chin and kissed her lightly. "Are you happy with your new home?"

Olivia lifted an arm to his neck to keep his mouth on hers. "How did you know I always wanted to live near the beach?"

Ellis kissed her and then gently set her away from him before it got out of hand. "Just a lucky guess. Selena is still sad we moved, but now she says they can use the house for a nanny when they decide to have kids. I think the baby bug is about to strike."

Olivia let him go and turned back to the crowd. She had been a little disappointed when she found out she wasn't pregnant but relieved at the same time. Right after she had moved into his home, he had told her he was thinking they should think about moving into a place of their own, away from prying eyes. Olivia truly liked Selena and Carter but was happy to be moving someplace that offered a bit more privacy. When Ellis had shown her the house he had in mind, she'd fallen in love with it. She could walk right out their back door and see the ocean any time she wanted. Though the house was not on the water, she had an ocean view and could lounge in her new swimming pool any time she felt like it and could see it from her backyard.

She knew one day she and Ellis would bring a child into their new home, but for now, Olivia was happy to have her husband all to herself. She had loved once, but it had been fleeting. Ellis had loved once, but the love had fallen away. When she asked him if he was sure about getting married and moving into a new home, he simply kissed her and told her that she was his forever love and there was nothing else in the world that he wanted more than to spend the rest of his days with her. She had cried happy tears at his sincere words and knew he was right. She knew that no matter what life brought them throughout their lives together, he was and would always be her forever love.

<h1 style="text-align:center">Books by Elizabeth Castle</h1>

Single Titles:
    Going Home
    This Kind Of Love
    Chasing Hope
    The Babe & The Librarian (novella)

The Heart's Way Series:
    For Now and Always
    Ask Me To
    Say You Love Me
    Forever Love

All Of Me Series:
    All Of My Days
    All Of My Nights

Bennett Family Series:
    This Time Love
    A Bride For David
(novella)

Cantwell Series:
    Falling Slowly
    Unraveled
    Hidden Away
    Entangled

Contemporary "Retro" Romance Series:
    Loving Jordan

Visit elizabeth-castle.com for newsletter sign up and up-to-date releases.